LET'S HEAR IT FROM A REAL SPITFIRE!

Angela saw Michael Harrison walking toward them carrying two cans of soda. His face, when he saw Pepper sitting beside her, lost its smile. He handed one coke to Angela.

"Tuckerman," he acknowledged curtly. "If you'll excuse us . . ."

"No, Harrison, *you* excuse *us!*" Pepper got up, and he and Mickey stood almost toe to toe, glaring at each other.

"*Dios mío!*" yelled Angela furiously. "The pair of you arguing over me like both of you have some *rights!* Like I got nothing to say about it! Well listen up! *Nobody* owns a piece of Angela Torres except Angela Torres!" And with those exasperated words, she ran off.

"*Ay, mi madre!*" She laughed to herself. "They are all alike, boys! Who would have thought that a couple of Wonder Bread preppies would have the same *machismo* in their souls as Sam Figueroa!"

HEARTS & DIAMONDS # 3

THE WRONG NAME FOR ANGELA

by

Leonore Fleischer

A SIGNET VISTA BOOK

NEW AMERICAN LIBRARY

NAL BOOKS ARE AVAILABLE AT QUANTITY DISCOUNTS WHEN USED TO PROMOTE PRODUCTS OR SERVICES. FOR INFORMATION PLEASE WRITE TO PREMIUM MARKETING DIVISION, NEW AMERICAN LIBRARY, 1633 BROADWAY, NEW YORK, NEW YORK 10019.

RL6/IL8+

SIGNET VISTA TRADEMARK REG. U.S. PAT. OFF. AND FOREIGN COUNTRIES REGISTERED TRADEMARK—MARCA REGISTRADA HECHO EN CHICAGO, IL., U.S.A.

SIGNET, SIGNET CLASSIC, MENTOR, PLUME, MERIDIAN and NAL BOOKS are published by New American Library, 1633 Broadway, New York, New York 10019

First Printing, April, 1986

1 2 3 4 5 6 7 8 9

PRINTED IN THE UNITED STATES OF AMERICA

For D.N.M., wherever you are

HOLLY HILLS

♥

When Holly Hills was founded, back in 1830, as a private boarding school for young ladies of good family, it was years ahead of its time. Although its students learned all the accomplishments expected of Victorian girls—music, painting on fans and china, fine needlework and Bible—also emphasized was the importance of the mind. Included in the Holly Hills curriculum were mathematics, geography, history, Latin, Greek, French, German, the less bawdy of the English poets, and fine penmanship, which today might be called "penpersonship."

The twentieth century has caught up with Holly Hills. The girls now elect to take computer science, feminist literature, short story writing, modern dance and classical ballet, pottery, theater, driver education, modern marriage, and archeology, as well as the usual science and humanities courses. A liberal scholarship program has brought girls from every economic walk of life to Holly Hills. But one thing hasn't changed. To be known as a Holly Hills girl you have to be smart and work hard. As a reward, the Holly Hills graduate is gladly accepted by every good university and college in America.

Holly Hills is a girls' school, true, but it's surrounded by boys' schools, the nearest one, Chatham, being only six miles away. Tucked into the rolling Connecticut countryside, surrounded by bushes of evergreen, Holly Hills offers crisp autumns and tender springs, deep white winters with sleigh rides and skating parties, and many opportunities for falling in love. Especially for falling in love . . .

CHAPTER ONE

The New Girl

On the first day that Angela Torres came to Holly Hills, she already had three strikes against her. First, she entered the school as a sophomore, one whole year too late to get in on and become a part of the friendships and new relationships that are formed in the freshman year. In freshman year, room assignments are made according to some mysterious system by Miss Appleyard—the headmistress—herself; but the sophs choose their own roomies, from among the classmates they have drawn close to in those first delicate and difficult months. Any new girl had to choose her roomie from among the leftovers, the poor rejects whom no soph of any importance had lowered herself to select.

Next, Angela Torres' looks and the way she dressed were certainly a strike against her. Holly Hills' dress code was not a strict one, except for chapel on Sunday, when a skirt, polished shoes, and panty hose were compulsory. Otherwise, a girl could pretty much wear what she wanted to class, as long as her body was decently covered.

But what most of the girls at Holly Hills wanted to wear was almost a uniform: a cashmere or Shetland sweater over designer jeans or pleated skirts. There were exceptions, of course. Artistic or super-fashionable girls often turned up in original outfits. Electra Minadou, for example, almost always dressed in black, and wore flaring miniskirts over black dance tights. But Electra was a dancer with a long, spare dancer's body, and she was so

7

exotic that she could get away with almost anything. Angela Torres just looked *alien*.

For instance, she wore high-topped sneakers. Not Adidas, Reebok, Ellesse—the status running shoes all athletic girls threw on the floor of their closets—but ordinary ratty old high-topped Keds, the kind inner-city boys wear when they're going one-on-one on the basketball court in a public playground.

"They're so . . . so . . . oooogie," said Missy Farina, wrinkling up her button of a nose and looking down with satisfaction at her own little feet, neatly shod in new Bass Weejuns, the pennies in them burnished to a pink copper glow. "And she wears them with those horrible mesh stockings! Black lace! I mean, I *mean*!"

"And her *hair*! Have you looked at her hair?" chimed in Jennifer Ripley, self-consciously smoothing down her soft, pale, mercifully straight locks. "It's inhuman!"

Angela Torres' hair was so thick and curly it was almost impossible to get a comb through it. It stood up in all directions in a black-tangled cloud. Her small, olive-skinned face appeared to be surrounded by a black forest from which dangled large golden hoops, gypsy earrings.

"And where did she get those *clothes*?" demanded Stacey Underhill, glancing for approval, as had the other two, at Anthea Tuckerman. "She looks like a fugitive from a rummage sale."

"Tucker" Tuckerman narrowed her jade-green cat's eyes and said nothing. But you could tell that she was thinking about Angela Torres' ragbag appearance by the disdainful half smile that played around her gorgeous lips.

Angela Torres had been seen on campus wearing full, swirling skirts of rayon, printed with large, bright tropical flowers, over which she wore tight T-shirts. In her first week at Holly Hills, she walked around with nothing on under the T-shirt, and the nipples of her high, round breasts could be seen quite plainly under the stretchy fabric. It wasn't until Miss Appleyard, known to all students as the Apple, had sent for her and spoken to her discreetly in her book-lined private study that Angela Torres, shrugging with indifference, had put on a bra.

And that was the third strike against her. Angela Torres' indifference was uncomfortably close to contempt. She didn't care what anybody thought—not about her clothes, her hair, her nipples, or her high-topped sneakers. She didn't even care who her roommate was to be, although they'd have to live together for a year. Since she had no preference and nothing to base a preference on, Miss Appleyard had made the assignment, just as though Angela Torres was a freshman.

The Apple put her into a tiny back room in Laurel Dorm with a mouse of a girl, Sara Grundfest, a born bookworm. Shy and timid Sara had hoped and prayed she'd be alone this year, and had sighed silently to herself when she saw the tall, flamboyant girl stalk in with a thundercloud brow. Angela Torres was larger than life and twice as vivid.

"Um, hi," whispered Sara, feeling an instant headache building behind her eyes.

Not bothering to reply, Angela Torres had given another of her signature shrugs and unpacked her single small suitcase. Angela Torres appeared to have what Miss Appleyard thought of privately as "a chip on her shoulder," but which the girls of Holly Hills called "an attitude." Like the Cat That Walked by Himself in the Kipling story, Angela Torres found that "all places were alike to her" and went entirely her own way. Anybody who got in her face was handed attitude, and usually got out of the way double quick.

Naturally, the more Angela Torres ignored the other Holly Hills girls, the more they talked about her and the more interest they showed in her appearance and her doings. Because she didn't give a damn whether her schoolmates were curious about her or not, her schoolmates were curious, even the seniors. Where did she come from? What had given her that touch-me-not attitude? Most important, what was a girl like Angela Torres doing at Holly Hills? She didn't "fit the profile," as Miss Appleyard might say.

Jennifer Ripley, who stuck her nose into everything, hung around the records office for a week, sneaking peeks into the file cabinets whenever nobody was looking. As soon as she had pieced together a few of the facts about Angela Torres' life before Holly Hills, she came running to Tucker Tuckerman with the information.

"She's Puerto Rican," she told Tucker breathlessly. "From the South *Bronx*! You know the movie with Paul Newman, *Fort Apache*? Well, that's where she comes from! And you'll never guess what!"

"No," drawled Tucker Tuckerman, looking bored as she almost always did, "but you no doubt are all aquiver to tell me."

"She's got a *record*! A *police* record! She was busted!"

Even Anthea Tuckerman's cat-green eyes, usually half shut and hooded, snapped open at *that* tidbit. "Indeed," she said softly, half to herself. "What did she do?"

Jennifer Ripley squirmed a little uncomfortably under the jade laser of Tucker Tuckerman's gaze.

"It . . . it . . . didn't say. There was a separate paper on that in the file, but it was stapled shut and I couldn't get a look at it."

"Wonderful, Ripley. The best part and you couldn't get a look at it. And *did* it say what Miss Ten-Most-Wanted is doing here at our beloved and exclusive school?"

"Well, she's apparently some kind of math genius or something. You know she's enrolled in Professor Woodstein's special differential calculus class, and that's usually open only to seniors in the math honors program. She's also taking private tutorials with him."

Thinking, Tucker tapped her perfect teeth with a perfect fingernail. One of the most admired students at Holly Hills, she combined beauty, brains, and breeding into an enviable package. Her great-grandfather had been a Supreme Court justice, her uncle Clarkson was a state senator, and one of her direct ancestors had been a signer of the Declaration of Independence. But other Tuckermans had been loyal to King George and had fought in the Revolution on the Tory side. One of them, Nahum Josiah

Tuckerman, had even been captured by the rebels and hanged; the family was especially proud of him. Tuckermans had sailed to America some four or five years *before* the *Mayflower* and had acted like lords and ladies of creation ever since.

Anthea Tuckerman had grown up in an atmosphere of wealth and quiet distinction, the sort of wealth where nothing one owns, not a tennis racquet or a Rolls-Bentley, is new. Old is good; new is bad. The most ancient part of the Tuckerman family home had been built by Dutch settlers in upstate New York in the late 1600s, had been added onto in 1743, and enlarged and made grand by the Tuckermans of the 1830s; they still referred to that wing as "the new house."

Tucker Tuckerman wore hand-me-downs. She wore simple gold earrings that had been handed down by her great-great-grandmother; a gold-and-enamel necklace that had once belonged to the Empress Josephine and had been handed down through the family until it reached Tucker. Someday, Tucker would hand it down to her own daughter. In her mother's safe-deposit box were other hand-me-downs, including some genuine pearls for her college graduation and some flawless diamond stud earrings that were to be forked over to Tucker on her wedding day.

Naturally, one never called attention to these things; it would be considered gauche, the worst possible manners. One wore one's things very casually, never displaying the labels in the sweaters (Turnbull & Asser, Jermyn Street, London S.W. 1) or in the polished loafers (Peale of Bond Street). One never but *never* wore or carried or toweled off with or slept on anything with initials on it, not one's own initials and certainly not one's designer's! Initials and monograms were a mark of new money. Therefore, they were to be despised.

And if all that weren't enough, Anthea Tuckerman was slim and blond and drop-dead beautiful, with perfect white teeth, fingernails which were *buffed,* not polished, those famous cat eyes, and the thinnest ankles in the sophomore and junior classes combined. The only slimmer ankles in all of Holly Hills belonged to a senior, Princess Ulumba of Ngorolo, but she had Watusi blood, standing seven feet high and weighing only 138 pounds. So the royal ankles hardly counted.

And if all *that* weren't enough, Anthea Tuckerman had a twin brother, Pepper Tuckerman, and he was to die for. Also a green-eyed blond, but with muscles, Pepper was enrolled in Cumberland Prep, one of the numerous brother schools that formed a ring around Holly Hills, thank heaven.

As popular and admired at Cumberland as Tucker was at Holly Hills, Pepper was constantly introducing his sister and her closest friends to attractive and important boys from Cumberland. Pepper himself was a notable prom-trotter and had been known to travel as far as Boston just to attend a junior hop at the most exclusive girls' school in Massachusetts.

Was it any wonder then that half the sophomore class at Holly Hills cosied up to Anthea Tuckerman? *Cosied up to* is a kind way to put it. *Sucked up to* would be more accurate. Especially Missy Farina and Jennifer Ripley and Stacey Underhill, who followed Tucker around like puppy dogs, begging for a pat on the head from that aristocratic Tuckerman hand. And for crumbs from the never-ending abundant Tuckerman feast of boys, boys, boys. Tucker went through boys like a hot knife through butter, melting them and casting them aside. Missy, Jennifer, and the boy-crazy Stacey hung around her, hoping to catch the discards and the leftovers rebounding off the backboard.

"Let me see if I have this straight," Tucker Tuckerman said coolly to Jennifer Ripley. "You're telling me that Angela what's-her-name-Rodriguez—"

"Torres," interrupted Missy Farina helpfully, but was mowed down for her trouble by an icy stare from her idol.

"—was arrested before coming to *Holly Hills*? Holly Hills, cherished academy which sends its seniors on to the Halls of Ivy and the Seven Sisters, not Kansas Land Grant Agricultural or Nowhere U.? Holly Hills, to which my father makes out a check every year for ten thousand dollars in tuition alone? Not to mention room and board and textbooks and those sweet little extras we all cannot live without, such as riding and tennis and pottery and aerobics and modern dance?''

''Uh-huh,'' agreed Jennifer. ''And she served time too.''

''How long?'' demanded Tucker.

''Six months. At a 'low-security correctional,' it said in her file.''

''Then presumably her crime was not murder or armed robbery. What a relief! Having paid her debt, having been restored to society, she was promptly shipped here to Holly Hills. I wonder why? These hallowed halls are no halfway house, yet she's enrolled in a senior honors math program even though a sophomore. I wonder what her story is. It should be an interesting one, maybe even fascinating. . . .'' Tucker Tuckerman's tone was thoughtful.

''She's getting extra tutorials from Woodstein too. She's taking a total of eight credits in math.'' Jennifer Ripley was a walking encyclopedia of useful information.

Anthea Tuckerman's cat eyes were now so narrow that almost no jade-green light escaped her lids. The pale-pink-pointed fingernail continued to tap her teeth thoughtfully, while Jennifer Ripley, Stacey Underhill, and Missy Farina sat enthralled, waiting for the verdict, at the foot of Tucker's perfectly made bed. Tucker had brought her own sheets to school, pearly white and pure linen, no monograms.

''Evidently the girl is something of a genius,'' said Tucker at last. ''And I rather like the way she looks. She has style.''

''Style! *Style!*'' The three of them reeled in astonishment.

Style was a sacred word in the Tuckerman set, and only Anthea Tuckerman was privileged to decide who possessed it and who didn't. Her word was law.

''But Tucker,'' protested Jennifer, ''she's so flashy! She looks like some gypsy fortune-teller!''

"She has *style,*" repeated Tucker more firmly. "She sounds interesting. I want to meet her. Arrange it, Ripley. You bring her to me."

Stacey and Missy breathed silent sighs of relief that Tucker hadn't laid this on them, while Jennifer Ripley closed her eyes and vowed never, *never* to mind anybody else's business again as long as she lived. Or was allowed to live. Here she was, firmly trapped between the rock and the hard place, and her own big mouth had put her there.

The hard place was Angela Torres, who was already notorious for scowling at anybody who dared to approach her and stalking off without a word. But suppose this time she didn't stalk? Suppose that arrest—for whatever offense—involved a weapon of some kind, put to some violent use or other? Suppose Angela Torres was still in possession of that weapon?

What could Jennifer say to her? "Uh, pardon me, but Tucker Tuckerman wants me to fetch you to her, like a dog or a package?" Or, "Tucker thinks you have style and wants to meet you. You're under arrest. Come along quietly with me now?"

Through closed eyes, Jennifer could picture clearly that dreadful scowl, those scornful eyes, those hoop earrings showing through the tangled curly hair. All she has to do is look at me cross-eyed and I'll run for my life! she thought.

But if Angela Torres was the hard place, Anthea Tuckerman was the rock. It had cost Jennifer too much brown-nosing and too much sweat just to get where she was now, barely tolerated by Tucker and her pals but definitely on the fringe of the friendship. And Jennifer Ripley had social aspirations; she dreamed of being accepted into the Tuckerman inner circle, one of the most exclusive cliques in the school and certainly *the* most exclusive in the sophomore class.

Already Jennifer could imagine future football weekends at Andover and Choate and Lawrenceville. Winter carnivals, senior proms, sleigh-riding parties, beach picnics. Someday they would all be hers if she could only worm her way into Anthea Tuckerman's good graces and stay there. Senior girls at Holly Hills were allowed to accept invitations like that, within reason, of course. Even juniors enjoyed somewhat relaxed rules about dating, and junior bliss was only a year away.

And all she had been asked to do was deliver the toughest girl in school to the richest and most influential. Wrapped in ribbons.

Lucky Jennifer!

CHAPTER TWO

Sam

Angela Torres marched into her room with that long-legged stride of hers and tossed her books onto the bed. Her mind was still whirling with the elegant intricacies of her mathematics tutorial. Theorems, hypotheses, and proofs continued to dance a minuet in her brain to a marvelously precise music. Professor Woodstein had set her a new and extremely difficult math problem to work out; Angela was already turning it over in her head, trying to puzzle out which angle to attack the problem from.

Sara Grundfest looked up from the Horace poem she was translating into English and smiled shyly at her roommate. As usual, her fingers were smudged with ballpoint ink and some of the smudges had transferred themselves to her beaky little nose, on which rested a pair of thick eyeglasses.

"Um, hi, Angela."

Angela returned her roommate's greeting with her customary nod and grunt. Sara was all right, for a squirt. At least she kept her mouth shut most of the time, which was more than Angela could say for the rest of this crappy school. How she had ever allowed herself to get into this situation—of being just about the only Hispanic in a collection of three hundred Barbie-doll idiots—well, it galled her just to think about it.

There were two other Spanish-speaking girls here, but both of them were from rich families in Spain, and they spoke a pure Castilian that sounded foreign to Angela's ears. Her own Spanish was salty with street expressions, mingled with English slang, a sort of "Spanglish." Besides, the Castilians snubbed Angela entirely, determined not to be associated in their schoolfellows' minds with this upstart from the South Bronx. Which was okay with Angela Torres. She wasn't losing any sleep over Amelia Herrera y Ramos or Mercedes Garcia-Moreno. Screw 'em and the limousines they rode in on. She had less use for them than they did for her.

Angela Torres had never wanted to come to Holly Hills in the first place, or the second place, either. But she'd had no choice. Her back had been to the wall. She'd already been in bad trouble once; if she didn't accept this full scholarship, she might be in worse trouble now.

"I don't want it," she'd told her grade adviser over and over. "Tell them to take that damn scholarship, roll it small, and stick it where the king don't roller-skate."

"It's the chance of a lifetime, Angela. You can't afford to turn it down," said Mrs. Deegan earnestly. "Besides, you yourself signed the application for it."

"Yeah, but only to get you off my case. I never thought for one minute they'd actually give it to me. Whatsa matter, they hurtin' for minorities? Am I trapped to be the token Hispanic?"

Palabras verdaderas. True words, man.

"What is it you want, Angela? Look me in the eyes and tell me that you don't want a really decent education, that you don't want to pursue your aptitude for math and see how far it takes you. Tell me that you have no goals in life and no ambitions. If you can say that to me truthfully, I'll tear the Holly Hills letter up right now."

But Angela, who never lied, couldn't tell Mrs. Deegan that. Because she did have goals, and ambitions, although she kept them secret. It was only that somehow . . . she wanted to believe that she might be able to achieve them alone, with no help from anybody. Fat chance! But Holly Hills! What kind of goofy name was that for a school? She gave an expressive heave to her supple shoulders and sighed loudly and dramatically.

"Connecticut. Shit! That's a million miles away from

New York, man! I'll tell you one thing true, it damn well better be a better school than Bronx Science or I'm takin' the first bus back.''

Mrs. Deegan reached over and patted Angela's hand. ''It's a different kind of world for you, Angela,'' she told her softly. ''It could mean a new start, getting out of New York City. Who knows, you might even like it.''

''Bull!'' Angela pulled her hand away angrily, feeling betrayed. She knew that Mrs. Deegan had been in conference with Mr. Ryan, Angela's corrections officer. Ryan and Deegan must have cooked this whole damn thing up together.

Being shipped off to some sissy girl's school in Connecticut was not what Angela Torres had in mind. It was like one of those lying phrases—*correctional facility* or *juvenile detention,* which was the *Norteamericano* fancy name for *reform school.* Angela Torres knew all about schools. She had been one of the rulers of her Bronx intermediate school, stalking like a soldier through its halls, head held high. And they'd all respected her. Smaller kids—mere *niños*—had come to her for help and advice, and she had always befriended them, protected them. Why?

Cause she was Angela Torres, that's why, man! Now she was being sent away again, and who knows what lies they had told her about Holly Hills?

Yet it had been Mrs. Deegan who had first perceived something far more important in Angela than her big rep or junior-high-school status. It had been Mrs. Deegan who had sponsored the series of scholastic-aptitude and intelligence tests at New York University and uncovered the phenomenal brain under that mass of curly black hair. When it came to mathematics, Angela Torres was a certifiable genius. She was not only a lightning calculator, but she had an incredible grasp of more abstruse mathematical concepts.

But what to do with her, that was the problem. With one or two possible exceptions, there was no high school in New York good enough in its math department to cultivate a mind like Angela's. And Mrs. Deegan refused to allow that mind to go to waste.

Years ago, Mrs. Deegan herself had been a student at Holly Hills, and she remembered its demanding curriculum with mingled fear and fondness. Today, Professor Charles Woodstein taught mathematics there. *The* Charles Woodstein, the man who, while at the Institute for Advanced Study at Princeton, had stumbled upon a proof so elegant that scholarly papers were still being written about it.

At seventy-five, the mathematician was now too old to continue with the full burden of teaching and had "retired" to Holly Hills, where he held advanced seminars for only the finest math students the school could offer. It was far less taxing than Princeton. The world of mathematics considered it an honor to be chosen for one of his classes, and it was this honor that Mrs. Deegan went after for Angela Torres.

Mrs. Deegan had telephoned Miss Appleyard, explaining all about Angela Torres and her incredible abilities, but not excluding a complete rundown of the trouble she'd been in.

Miss Appleyard had sounded somewhat doubtful. "She certainly doesn't fit the usual profile of the Holly Hills student," she said slowly. "Not even of the usual scholarship student."

"No, she certainly doesn't," agreed Mrs. Deegan. "Angela doesn't fit the usual profile of anybody or anything. But she's worth it, worth any amount of difficulty, any amount of adjustment on her part or the school's. You'll see. She's rebellious, true, and ferociously independent, but Angela Torres is one in a million; I've never encountered another student like her. Besides everything else, she has true integrity."

There was a moment's silence on the phone as Miss Appleyard considered. Then she said briskly, "If Professor Woodstein agrees, I'll take her."

"It will have to be a full scholarship—tuition, board,

textbooks, everything. The family doesn't have a dime," warned Mrs. Deegan.

"Now why am I not surprised to hear that?" the Apple sighed.

As difficult as it was for Angela to make up her mind to accept Holly Hills' offer of a full scholarship, it was twice as hard telling her boyfriend Sam.

They'd been going together for almost two years now; ever since Angela was fourteen years old and had first laid eyes on him. Since then, it had been Angela-and-Sam, as though you were saying only one word. Which, in a way, you were.

But telling Sam she was going away and getting Sam to accept it were two entirely different matters.

"Connecticut! Are you loco, man?" he'd shouted at her when she broke the news about Holly Hills and its scholarship. "You know how far that is from the Bronx?"

"One hundred and twenty four miles; exactly two hours and fourteen minutes on your Kawasaki if the traffic isn't bad." Angela tried to sound flippant, but failed miserably. She knew by heart, down to the quarter mile, the distance that would be separating her from Sam.

"Damn it, Angela," he said more quietly, his handsome dark face brooding, "I thought you loved me. Now you tell me you want to go away."

"I *do* love you, baby," she assured him unhappily. "And I *don't* want to go away; I'd much rather stay with you. But don't you see, this is my chance! A chance to make something of myself, a chance to study with one of the best brains in the field, to learn—" Unconsciously, she repeated Mrs. Deegan's arguments.

"What the hell do you have to learn for, when the two of us are gonna get married and have babies? You're supposed to stay here with me and your family, not with some nutty professor and a bunch of stinking rich *muchachas*!" Sam's mouth set into a stubborn line, and he turned his back on her.

They were sitting, as they usually did when they wanted

to be alone, on the roof of Angela's apartment building on Anderson Avenue in the South Bronx. It was late June; in a few days school would be over, and they'd have the summer together.

After that . . . Holly Hills.

Angela's heart was heavy; Sam's attitude hurt her in more ways than one. The fact that he couldn't fully accept her as his equal—that *he* was the one who was supposed to make the plans for their future while *she* should only tag along behind him—this assumption of his was something that always caused her pain. It was often the way things were in the South Bronx. Men made decisions and women made babies, but that's not what Angela saw as her own future. She wanted something more out of life, something positive, creative, important, fulfilling.

Angela Torres wanted a future in which marriage and babies would be a major and beloved part, yet be less than the whole. She wanted to do something on her own, and do it well, whatever it was. And she wanted to share it with Sam, her Sam.

Ismail Figueroa—Sam. Tall, handsome, with a smooth skin a shade or two darker than Angela's olive complexion. Beautiful Sam, built like a panther with long flanks and narrow hips, all his power in his shoulders and chest. Sam, with eyes like giant coffee beans, ringed by thick black curly lashes. He was a turn-on, and he knew it. When he flashed a dazzling white smile, his dark face lit up and a dimple at the left outer corner of his curved upper lip appeared and disappeared, like a wink. If his eyes had been blue instead of jet black, Sam would be a ringer for John Travolta, only younger and better looking.

Sam, how Angela loved him! When he'd sauntered into her classroom that day, two years ago, her heart had given such a jump that she almost fell out of her seat. He didn't have a room pass, he wasn't even supposed to be in the building because he was already in high school, but, outlaw that he was, he'd come looking for a friend, and had found instead—Angela.

He'd taken one look at that wild mop of black curls and

two huge brown eyes and foxy little body, and decided on the spot that his friend could keep. Hanging around the school yard at three, he'd spotted her coming out of the building, flanked by two girlfriends.

Sam looked her over with appreciation, noticing her long legs, unusual in a Puerto Rican girl, her broad, straight shoulders, and confident walk. Together with that wild gypsy hair and those eyes—*Ay, dios mío!* This girl really had something!

Getting her to talk to him was not easy. On either side of her, her girlfriends kept giggling slyly and poking each other, driving him nuts. Angela herself kept her cool, allowing only the tiniest little smile to play at the corners of her lips. In her pierced ears, two silver hoops danced, and so did her eyes. But she wouldn't say a word to Sam.

In truth, she didn't dare. Angela was much too nervous, scared out of her wits by his good looks and his incredible charm. On the outside, she was composed and confident. On the inside, she was a terrified little girl. She'd never had a real boyfriend; she was totally inexperienced, and this tall, good-looking guy just oozed cocky smoothness.

"Angela, my angel! An angel right out of heaven," he teased, elbowing one of the giggling girls out of the way and taking his place at Angela's side. "My angel, give me a little kiss! *Mi corazón, mi amor!* My soul is dying for you, Angela. Don't be a devil, be an angel! Oh, my heart! You're killing me, Angela! Help, murder, police!"

He was outrageous, clutching at his chest and pretending to stagger. Her friends were in convulsions, but Angela could not permit herself to look at him. One look and she would be lost. Already her heart was beating so loud she was afraid he'd hear it. She was falling in love with this boy, but she mustn't show it. So she kept her nose high in the air in order not to see that dimple and melt all over the sidewalk.

What if he were only kidding around? After all, he was a good two years older than she, already in high school, almost a man. She was still, in the eyes of the world, a little girl. Only fourteen. Tall, developed for her age, maybe, but still only fourteen. And he was so handsome he could have any girl he wanted. What if he was only putting her on? Suppose she were to stop right this minute and hold out her hand to him, would he take it? Or would he back off, shaking his head?

She was a proud girl, Angela Torres, and she was afraid to take the risk.

On the other hand, what if he *was* interested in her? After all, he had hung around the school yard until classes were over. Wasn't it Angela he had been waiting for? Didn't that mean something? Look at him playing the fool now, but was that for his own amusement or hers?

She yearned to be alone with Sam, so that she could look deeply into his face and see if he was telling the truth. Other girls could banter easily with boys, throwing mock compliments and mock insults back and forth with enjoyment. But not Angela. She was always serious, never spoke a word that wasn't the stone truth. And the stone truth was, she was already crazy about Ismail Figueroa.

They were out of the school yard now, and her girlfriends had moved off in the direction of their own homes, still giggling, envious of Angela and her new "boy." Angela stood there awkwardly, uncertain of what to do next, whether to stay or go.

"Want a lift home?" asked Sam.

She noticed how his hair was combed smooth, into a shining black cap, with one curl twisted and falling over his forehead. The rational part of her pointed out that the curl was contrived, guaranteed to be adorable to brainless girls. But the rest of her found the curl adorable.

"You drive?" she asked, surprised.

"That's"—and he pointed to a battered old Honda motorcycle, 350 cc, not much more than a scooter—"mine."

Angela had never been on a motorcycle before, and to her the little Honda looked big and dangerous. She couldn't wait to try it. "Sure, why not?"

Sam straddled the cycle and glanced over his shoulder. "Hop on. Now wrap your arms around me and hold tight."

Angela hesitated, then climbed onto the seat behind Sam, holding him loosely at the waist. Damned if she was going to wrap her arms around a total stranger, no matter how fantastic.

Turning the ignition on, Sam gave a little jump into the air and kick-started the Honda. Off they roared. Terrified, Angela flung her arms around him as tightly as she could and held on for dear life, her cheek pressed against Sam's leather jacket. She could feel him laughing at her, but she was too scared to be mortified.

"Where do you live?" His words were carried away by the wind and the roar of the motorbike's engine.

"Whaaat?"

"I said, where do you live?"

"Oh, on Anderson and 158th Street," she shouted back, and nestled her head down again against his leathers.

She'd never felt anything like this, this sensation of swiftness as the Honda wove in and out of traffic, dodging trucks and cars. She was flying; her hair streamed out behind her; the wind tore at her clothing. Only her face, pressed hard against Ismail Figueroa's back, was safe from the wind. This was frightening, this was wonderful, this was the only way to travel.

It seemed like only seconds, but it was at least ten minutes before they pulled up in front of Angela's apartment building. Shaky, she got off the bike reluctantly.

Sam took one look at the thin girl whose dark eyes were radiant, whose olive skin was made rosy by the wind. She was still shivering with cold. He laughed loudly. "You ought to get a look at yourself," was all he said. "Your hair looks like you combed it with an eggbeater."

Then he kick-started the Honda and zoomed off without another word.

Loping up the five flights to her top-floor apartment, Angela felt her pulses racing as she turned the key in the lock. Nobody was home; both her mother and father worked. Her older brothers and sisters were already married and out of the house, and her baby sister Rosita was at a day-care center.

She ran straight to the mirror in the tiny room that was hers and did a long survey of her reflection. He was right; the wind had taken her already tousled hair and churned it into a mess of truly astonishing proportions.

"Oh, damn! Damn! I look like what the cat threw up after breakfast!" she moaned, tugging viciously at her hair. "No wonder he laughed at me! I'll never see him again, I know it! Damn!"

CHAPTER THREE

Going Away

After she met him, Angela spent the next two days half expecting Sam to show up, and half hoping he wouldn't. She hated this new way she was feeling—nervous, dependent, her own life taken out of her own hands. If this is supposed to be love, I don't want it! she swore to herself.

Angela needed all her energy to stay ahead of her schoolwork; she was in an advance class where the demands on her were heavy, and so was her homework load. But every time she tried to concentrate, a pair of bright black eyes came dancing between her and the page, and a dimple flashed. As she sat writing out math equations in her neat handwriting, a whiff of Sam's leather jacket would steal into her imagination, and she would put down her pencil to lose herself in daydreams.

When Sam didn't show up or telephone her, Angela tried hard to put him out of her mind. But it was no use. Here was a boy she'd said hardly two words to, a boy she'd been with for less than half an hour, and all of a sudden he was the most important person in her life! Well, obviously he didn't feel that way about her. Or else he would have phoned.

It was a week before she saw him again. Leaving school at the end of the day, surrounded by her girlfriends, she heard Maria Concepcion giggle and say, "There's your boyfriend, Angela," and she looked up to find herself staring into those incredible black eyes, framed in thick lashes.

"C'mon, I'll drive ya home." He grabbed her by the

elbow, leading her to his motorcycle before she could open her mouth to protest.

When she saw the Honda, Angela gasped. Newly attached to the back of the saddle was a long bar in the shape of an inverted U—"sissy bars," created for a passenger to lean back on while riding behind the driver. And on the saddle itself was a small-size leather jacket and a brand-new shiny helmet of golden space-age material, with goggles attached. Emblazoned on the front of the helmet was one word—*Angela*. Sam had had this made especially for her!

"So ya don't look so messy," Sam had said coolly. "I hate a messy lady, especially on my bike. Also, so ya don't catch pneumonia or break your damn head and blame it on me. C'mon, what are ya waitin' for? Climb on!"

Climb on. That had been Sam's only declaration of love, but it was eloquent and romantic enough. Angela had climbed on two years ago, and they'd been together ever since. The old Honda had bitten the dust and been replaced by a hotshot Kawasaki, 650 cc, which Sam was still busting his butt making monthly payments on. The Kawasaki had a double saddle and fancier sissy bars, but Angela still preferred to ride with her arms tightly around Sam Figueroa's waist, her cheek pressed against the leather of his jacket.

They did so many things together, because the bike gave them freedom. With Sam's wheels, the richness of New York City was unfolded to Angela for the first time. They drove all the way down Manhattan into Brooklyn and across the Verrazano Bridge, to explore Staten Island. Angela had heard that somewhere on Staten Island was a genuine Buddhist temple with a garden of meditation, and she longed to see it. Sam had scoffed—in New York City? No way, José!

But they did find it together, on the bike, and it was every bit as beautiful and as peaceful as Angela had hoped. They had spent three hours in the temple gardens, saying nothing, just drinking in the tranquillity and holding hands. Sam didn't even light a cigarette, and Angela didn't want to smoke, because this place was so evidently holy.

They listened to music together—Latin, of course, but also Angela's favorites, progressive jazz, and rock'n'roll. They danced, moving well together whether they were slow-dancing or shaking their hips to the beat of salsa. Sam had all the moves. They looked good together, the tall boy and the slim girl almost as tall as he.

Every Saturday night they took in at least one movie, sometimes even two or three, gulping them down one after the other—old pictures, new ones, romance, chain-saw massacres, great classic films, campy trash—it almost didn't matter to the two of them, because they loved movies so much.

When Angela turned fifteen, Sam gave her her very first kiss. For months, she had wanted him to kiss her, dreamed about his holding her in his strong arms. But he'd kept his distance. He had rules for himself about everything, and he obeyed them strictly. You don't kiss fourteen-year-old girls; they're still babies. It wasn't a rule he was going to break, not even for Angela.

How impatiently she'd waited to turn fifteen! What incentive she had! On the morning of her fifteenth birthday, Angela awoke thinking *kiss*. She had a date with Sam that night, of course, and all day long she kept thinking about that first promised kiss.

She dressed up with special care, in the prettiest thing she owned, a new dark red jersey that showed off her blooming young figure. With the careful application of eyeliner and mascara, she made her eyes appear even wider and darker. With infinite patience—so unlike her usual self —Angela gathered her mop of hair together, smoothing it and sweeping it back from her face, pinning it with jeweled combs.

When she was finished, she took a long, satisfied look at herself. She really did look much older than fifteen— perhaps even eighteen! Sam could never think of her as a baby now. She had no idea where Sam would be taking her, but she was confident it would be somewhere special.

When he showed up that evening, in a new silky shirt

that clung to his chest and shoulders, the word *kiss* began hammering in Angela's brain. It was all she could do to keep from flinging herself into his arms.

"Hey, happy birthday, *guapa,* you look nice," he commented casually, but his eyes shone.

"You too, Sam. Where are we going?"

"Oh, I got a great place picked out for us. You'll see."

The great place turned out to be the roof of Angela's tenement building. The sky was vast and very dark, and a few stars managed to shine through the air pollution, which meant that somewhere out in the country, where the air was clean, it must be a fantastically starry night.

"Let's sit," said Sam Figueroa softly.

"But my new dress—" protested Angela.

"I'll pay for the cleaning. I got something for you."

Boy and girl sat down side by side on the grimy roof, and Sam pulled a little box out of his jacket pocket and placed it in Angela's hands. She opened it.

It was almost too dark to see, but the gleam of real gold came up from the little box, and her fingers traced the outlines of engraved hoop earrings.

"Oh, Sam, they're beautiful!" breathed Angela. "At least, they *feel* beautiful."

"Feliz cumpleaños, Angelita," he whispered back. "Happy birthday." Reaching out, he took her small face very gently into his hands, cupping it in his palms. Then he bent his head to hers.

Here it comes, the kiss! thought Angela, her heart thumping with excitement. It was the last rational thought she would have for several minutes.

His first kiss was gentle, barely the touch of a butterfly's wing, his lips grazing hers. Then his lips brushed over her cheeks, her brows, her eyelids and her hair. Sam kissed Angela's chin and nose, then he let his mouth meet hers again. This time he allowed the kiss to deepen, to seek. He allowed Angela to kiss him back.

From the first instant she'd set eyes on Sam, she'd wondered what it would feel like to have his lips on hers. What would she do? How would she kiss him back,

knowing nothing of kissing? Now that the moment was
here, her fears retreated and purest instinct took over. And
she kissed him as though her life depended on it, as though
she'd kissed him every day of her life.

It was wonderful. She was fifteen years old, and in love.
She was fifteen, in love and kissing the most desirable boy
in all the world. And it was her birthday, and he'd given
her gold hoop earrings for her pierced ears. What more
could life hold in store?

That's when they really began going steady, going every-
where together on the Kawasaki, spending all their free
time in each other's company. It really started between
them that night of her first kiss. That was the first time
that Angela was really certain of Sam's love.

Whenever they were alone, which wasn't often, they exchanged long, passionate, disturbing kisses. Angela felt
that she was far too young to go all the way with Sam,
although so often she was tempted to. She thought about it
a lot; it would mean a greater commitment on the part of
both of them and she didn't think she was ready for anything so heavy.

What she was really afraid of was getting pregnant, and
having to get married. A couple of her girlfriends were
already in that situation, married at fifteen, mothers at
sixteen. The freedom and wonder of life seemed to be over
for them; their lives weren't their own anymore; it was
wrapped up in Pampers and tied up with diaper pins.
Good-bye, independence. Angela vowed she'd never let
that happen to her. Besides, she was totally inexperienced.

Sam had already had many girlfriends, but Angela had
never known another boy, never even kissed a boy before
Sam. What kind of future did they have? At fourteen,
fifteen, sixteen, how could she be sure? So the two years
had passed with nothing more than kissing and a little
fooling around. Angela would always stop Sam in time.
She knew that Sam was normal and healthy, that he was
"getting it" somewhere else, from girls unknown to her.
Maybe one of those cooperative girls would snag him

permanently for herself, but that was just a risk Angela would have to take. Their relationship was too important to her. If she didn't trust him, she'd lose him anyway.

Sam belonged to a neighborhood club, Los Hidalgos, with a clubhouse. Just a basement, really, where no more than a dozen or so Hispanic boys got together to play penny poker, drink a little beer, and swap lies and brags. Some of them had dropped out of school and were working in nickel-and-dime jobs with no futures—pushing racks of dresses through busy Seventh Avenue traffic in the garment district or working as messengers and delivery boys.

"That will never be you!" Angela would tell him vehemently. "You're going to stay in school and graduate and go on to college! You're smart, Sam, and you're going to use that brain, because I won't allow you to let it go down the tubes!"

But Sam would only shrug and smile and change the subject. He had a favorite expression that he brought out from time to time. *Take the best and leave the rest.* Whatever it meant, it made Angela so furious she'd ball her little hands up into fists. Couldn't he see? Didn't he know? Education was the key to everything!

He loved her, though. In his own macho way, he showed it. He was there for her. Some evenings when it was too cold to go up on Angela's roof and the clubhouse was empty, they'd go down to Los Hidalgos and hide themselves in one another's arms, in a world of their own, a world that took Angela's breath away. More than once, she had come dangerously close to losing that independence of hers, and only an enormous effort of will had saved her.

And when the awful, unspeakable trouble came, and Angela was sent away to that terrible place and came out bitter, disillusioned, and angry, Sam was always there for her, trying in a thousand different ways to make it better, to kiss away the hurt. Now it was Angela who refused to talk about the possibilities of a future, and it was Sam who coaxed her with reminders that they would always be together. To Sam, the future always meant marriage with Angela.

But with the Holly Hills scholarship, all that was going to change, and Sam hated it. Angela had told him she didn't want to go away, but she was going away. She had told him she didn't care a damn about school anymore, but she was going more than a hundred miles away, just to learn advanced mathematics. To Sam, it just didn't make sense. Two people unhappy, and for what?

"Look, Angela, why don't we get married?" he asked her, as soon as she'd told him about Holly Hills.

"Married?" Her eyes snapped open in surprise. "Now? But I'm only sixteen!"

"My mother was sixteen when *she* got married, and only eighteen when I was born," Sam pointed out earnestly.

Yes, and now that she's thirty-six, she's a worn-out old woman. That's not for me—four kids before I'm twenty, thought Angela. But she didn't dare to say it out loud; she hated to hurt Sam.

"We'll see each other a lot, Sam," she promised. "If you don't come and get me on the bike, I swear I'll *walk* the hundred and twenty-four miles and grab you by the . . . ears," she finished, laughing. "It's not like I'm going to another planet."

"Yes it is, Angela." He grabbed her hands and held them tightly, forcing her to look him full in the face. "It *is* another planet for people like you and me. We don't belong there. We got nothing in common with them, and they don't want us. Stay here with me, *chicita*," he pleaded. "Stay in *our* world."

Angela had shaken her head sadly. "It's too late. But we still have the summer. We can be together all summer."

And they had; it had been a summer that both of them would remember all their lives, a summer of love, of hot, humid city days at the public beaches, of starry nights on Angela's roof, a summer of kisses and promises.

On their last day together, Sam's handsome face was

troubled, and his lips grim. Angela felt her heart cracking inside her; she couldn't stand the look in his eyes.

As if to echo their mood, it was raining—a long, slanting, gloomy rain that spoke of summer as only a memory and promised a long winter to come.

"Let's go to the clubhouse," urged Sam.

Angela shook her head. "What good would that do? It would just make it that much harder for me to leave you."

"No, c'mon. I got something to show you. A surprise."

"I'll just bet." Angela grinned. Sam Figueroa didn't grin back. His astonishingly large black eyes looked pleadingly into hers.

"Okay, let's go." She agreed.

They rode through the rain on Sam's motorbike, Angela shivering in her summer dress and sweater. At least the clubhouse would be warm and dry. Maybe there wouldn't be anybody there and they could snatch a last hour or two alone. Angela already ached with missing Sam.

But there *were* people in the Los Hidalgos clubhouse, dozens of them. Standing stunned in the doorway, Angela Torres gasped in astonishment.

Not only her friends, but also her parents were there! And her sisters and brothers with their husbands and wives, and Angela's little nieces and nephews. Angela blinked in disbelief. Mrs. Deegan, her grade adviser was there, and even Mr. Ryan her corrections officer. Kids from school, all of Los Hidalgos and their girlfriends, even *los pequenos,* the little kids whom Angela always befriended.

A crude paper banner, with *Buena Suerte, Angela Torres* painted across it in large red letters spanned the back of the room. Balloons filled with helium hung from the ceiling. A long table overloaded with bowls of food, platters of cold cuts, coolers of soda and beer, and gift-wrapped packages in bright patterned paper and ribbons had been set up in the middle of the room.

Everybody was talking and laughing at the same time, running toward Angela. She didn't know if she should laugh or cry, so she did a little of both, and a lot of hugging, so much hugging her shoulders and arms were soon tired.

She turned to Sam, but he wasn't there. He'd disappeared. But before she could ask for him, he reappeared, wheeling out something red and shiny and wonderful, wrapped in a wide white ribbon and tied in an enormous bow. Angela couldn't believe her eyes! A Honda Aero 50! It was the prettiest little motor scooter she'd ever seen, and there, on the saddle, was a brand-new helmet, with her name—Angela Torres—on it in a fancy, curly script.

"From me to you, *guapa*." Sam grinned. "I couldn't let my lady walk down some long cold hundred-twenty-four mile road."

"Dios mío!" gasped Angela. "It must have cost you a fortune!"

"I really wanted to get you the Elite 80, but I couldn't swing it," answered Sam ruefully. "But this also has push-buttons to start, and you don't have to shift. It's easier than a bicycle."

"But too much faster," put in Mrs. Torres. "*Niña,* you must promise me to drive it very, very carefully."

"Oh, I will, Mama," breathed Angela, perishing to get on and try it right away. "I love you," she said to Sam, and then, afraid she'd said too much in front of her family and friends, she turned to them. "I love you *all*!" She threw out her arms in a universal hug, as if embracing the entire room. "Thank you! Thank you! I'll try to make you proud of me!" she vowed.

Mrs. Deegan put one strong arm affectionately around Angela's shoulders. "We're already proud of you, dear, and I'm certain you will continue to make us proud. Bear in mind that this will probably be one of the most rich and wonderful opportunities of your life. Make the most of it."

"Yeah," put in Sam, his lips twisting wryly. "Remember what I always told you. *Take the best and leave the rest.*"

The next day Angela was on her way to Holly Hills,

riding her precious little Honda Aero, the wind whipping around her, catching at the curls that peeked out of the bottom of her brand-new helmet. She felt, suddenly, that life might be good after all, and that there might even be a pot of gold at the end of the Holly Hills rainbow.

How was Angela to know at that happy moment that it would turn out to be exactly as Sam had predicted—that Angela Torres would land on another planet? And except for her classes with Professor Woodstein, it would be a planet she hated, whose air she couldn't breathe.

CHAPTER FOUR

A.T.

Sara Grundfest knew that the rest of her class regarded her as a bookworm with no personality of her own, as somebody to be ignored. She had realized early in life that she wasn't going to grow up pretty or be attractive to boys. Sara tried to keep this realization from making her unhappy, and most of the time she succeeded. When she was nose deep in one of her beloved books, she managed to forget for a little while how cruel and indifferent the outside world could be when you hadn't been born pretty.

But whenever the outside world came knocking insistently at her door, Sara Grundfest forced herself to take a deep breath, square her small, rounded shoulders, and meet life head-on. In the school dining room, for example. She would have skipped meals entirely if she could, snacking on apples and cheese in her room, nourished by the poetry of Pindar and Catullus, of Shelley and Pope, but it was forbidden to miss a meal without a written excuse from the school doctor. Holly Hills was forever on guard against teenage anorexia.

So Sara would load up her tray with as little as she could get away with and go looking, her heart in her mouth, for an empty seat. None of the other girls at Holly Hills wanted to sit next to her; they all seemed to have somebody they were saving seats for and never thought twice about propping a chair against a table—signifying "taken"— whenever they saw Sara inching along. Nobody ever stopped to consider her feelings, if indeed Sara Grundfest had any feelings at all.

Oh, she did, she had feelings, but they were there, apparently, only to be hurt. Inside that ink-stained body beat the heart of a poet. Under those straggly braids was a mind of great delicacy and romantic vision. But what boy would ever make the effort to find that out, who would ever warm himself by the fire that burned in her soul? It seemed to her sometimes that she was doomed to live her life lonely and alone.

It wasn't that way at home. Sara Grundfest's mother and father were both scholars of high reputation—her mother an anthropologist, her father a translator of classical languages. They took great satisfaction from the brilliance of their only child. But they had been middle-aged when they'd had Sara, and they wouldn't live forever. Where would she go then? What doors would be open to her?

Sometimes Sara tried to picture her future in her own mind. She was convinced that she'd wind up as one of those virgin ladies who taught Latin at some small private academy. Her only love affair would be with Catullus, a poet dead for many centuries. Her only life companion would be a cat or perhaps a small, yappy dog. In either case, her tweed skirt would always be tufted with patches of shedding fur, and her old cardigan sweater would be worn thin at the elbows. Her students would make fun of her behind her back and give her cruel nicknames—Old Grundpest. Once every five years or so a brilliant student would cross her path, someone whose mind was worth nurturing. She'd recommend books and serve cups of China tea, while the cat (or the small, yappy dog) snoozed and snored in front of the little fireplace in her room. But the student would graduate and take his or her rightful place in the world, leaving Old Grundpest behind, and would never write or phone the old teacher again.

This dismal picture of the future was hardly what Sara really wanted. Sara Grundfest longed to drink wine and dance naked in the moonlight at the temple of Diana at Ephesus. Sara Grundfest yearned to be swept away to safety at the very last minute by a handsome Sir Lancelot, leaving the dragon frustrated and quite dead behind her. She wanted to perch high on the saddle behind him, her cheek cold against his armor. She wanted to be tall. She wanted to be beautiful. She wanted to conquer worlds. She wanted to be like Angela.

Angela Torres was everything Sara Grundfest admired. Not only was she exotically beautiful, but she was angry —her eyes flashed like the goddess Athene's, the pavements buckled under her stride, her lovely lips curled in majestic contempt. Angela Torres was a revolutionary, an outlaw who cared nothing for the outdated conventions of the school. Angela Torres was alone because she *chose* to be alone, because she saw nobody around her worthy of her friendship. Angela Torres was a genius at mathematics. Angela Torres had a lover. Not an insipid, pale "boyfriend," but a macho, darkly handsome Spanish lover who wanted to marry her. Sara knew that from overhearing her roommate's telephone conversations. Not that she was voluntarily eavesdropping, but the hallway phone *was* right outside their room, and Angela never bothered to lower her voice.

Sara knew that Angela hadn't chosen her as roommate. Nobody had chosen her, but she had expected that. Yet she was grateful that it was Angela whom the Apple had put in with her. Because, while Angela ignored Sara in the same way that she ignored everybody, Angela didn't torment her. She never teased her or made fun of her, not like Jennifer Ripley or Stacey Underhill or Missy Farina, who were always brownnosing Anthea Tuckerman by making mockery of *creeps* and *turkeys* and *nerds* like Sara.

Even though Angela Torres didn't know it, Sara had secretly sworn eternal friendship and undying loyalty to Angela Torres. When she had read Aesop's fable of the lion and the mouse, she thought of herself and Angela, hoping that some day she, like the mouse in the fable, could prove helpful to her lioness of a roommate.

Of all the girls at Holly Hills, only Sara Grundfest recognized that Angela Torres was, deep inside, unhappy.

The opposite side of the coin of ferocious independence is often self-enforced loneliness, and Angela was lonely.

Apart from her beloved mathematics, there seemed to be nothing and nobody to bind Angela to Holly Hills or her schoolmates. She had no friends, but took great care to look as though she didn't miss or want them. Yet Sara suspected otherwise. She suspected that Angela wanted a friend badly, and wished with all her little bookworm heart that it could be she.

Angela didn't enjoy any of her other subjects or take part in any of the school's other activities. Not music, or drama, or sports. Even with her long legs and athletic body, she despised sports and didn't show up for any. This was painful to the P.E. teacher, Ms. Wyner, who, after watching Angela Torres shinny up a gym-class rope in nothing flat, was desperate to have her competing on a school team. When Wyner had seen Angela's high-top Keds, hope had been born in her heart. But Angela had killed that hope with one disdainful shrug.

It was ironic; here was Angela Torres with everything that Sara Grundfest wished she had, and Angela was no less miserable than Sara herself. Both of them misfits, loners, outcasts.

As Angela now skimmed through the few pieces of mail she'd taken from her mailbox, Sara turned back to the Latin poem she was translating as homework. A sudden exclamation from Angela made her look up again.

In her hand Angela was holding a large, white envelope; across the front was scrawled initials large enough for even nearsighted Sara to see from across the room. "A.T."

"What the hell—?" Angela ripped the envelope open and read its contents aloud.

"Hi! You're invited, of course, to join us for Midnight Munchies in my room Wednesday night. Missy's mother baked Scotchies and blondies, and Stacey has been stashing a canned ham, the greedy piggy! Love, Jennifer.' Who the hell is Jennifer?" Angela looked truly mystified. "And what's a Missy or a Stacey?"

It was instantly clear to Sara, but she hesitated, unsure of whether Angela had been actually talking to *her* or just wondering out loud. "Ummm . . ." She cleared her throat nervously.

"You got the answer?" demanded Angela, turning to her roommate.

Sara took her glasses off and polished them on a corner of her blouse, her habit when nervous. "I . . . I *think* . . ."

"You think what? Come on, spit it out!"

"I think you got that note by mistake. I think it was meant for Anthea Tuckerman. The two of you have the same initials, A.T. Jennifer Ripley is a good friend of hers, and so are Missy Farina and Stacey Underhill. It must have been put in the wrong box."

Angela nodded; it made perfect sense. If the note wasn't for her . . . she started to rip it up. Then she shrugged, thinking better of it. It wasn't her property to destroy.

"Who the hell is this Andrea Tuckerman?" she asked Sara.

"Anthea. Tucker Tuckerman, the blonde in the expensive sweaters? She's in our English class."

"The one who goes around looking like she's smelling shit all the time?"

Catullus himself couldn't have put it better, thought Sara. "That's her."

Angela tapped the letter against her cheek. I owe her zip; I'm not her delivery boy, she thought, but she knew that the only right thing to do was to bring the letter to its real owner and explain why it had been opened. "Where does she hang out?"

"She's in our dorm, on the second floor. The big front room, of course." Sara couldn't help adding the *of course*.

"I'm out of here."

Jennifer isn't as dumb as I'd imagined, thought Tucker as she accepted the opened letter and Angela's explanation with a gracious smile.

The ploy of the letter was instantly transparent to Tucker Tuckerman. It was Jennifer Ripley's way of carrying out her assignment without having to approach the dreaded Angela Torres face-to-face. But Scotchies, blondies, and canned ham! Tucker's genteel tummy turned a bit queasy at the thought. The only thing Anthea Tuckerman had ever eaten out of tins was fresh caviar, and she never touched sugar in any form. Still, score a point for Jennifer; the letter had done its job. It had delivered Angela Torres to Anthea Tuckerman, as ordered.

"Won't you sit down for a few minutes and visit with me?" invited Tucker. "I hear such wonderful things about you that I've really been looking forward to meeting you."

Instantly, Angela Torres was on her guard. What wonderful things? She looked around. This must easily be the best room in Laurel Dorm; it was certainly the biggest. And even though it was furnished exactly as all the others were—two plain beds, two chests of drawers with mirrors, two desks, two chairs—Angela's sharp senses detected subtle differences.

For one thing, the room *smelled* different. Not of dusty furniture and old sneakers, but of scented candles. The sheets on one of the beds were of a startling whiteness and purity; Angela guessed correctly that this was Tucker's bed. The photos on one of the bureaus were in solid silver frames, and there was a matching set of silver-backed brushes, a silver-encased comb, and some weird-looking instrument that Angela didn't recognize, a nail buffer. Hanging at the windows were curtains of the sheerest linen, letting in light without obstructing the lovely view of the holly bushes and the hills beyond. There were other little touches too that Angela's brain didn't bother to catalog, but which all added up to one word—*money*.

And here was the queen of the universe, decked out in tweed and cashmere and smelling of Floris eau de cologne, her golden hair brushed as flat and smooth as a bolt of silk, waving one manicured hand and inviting her to sit down.

Well, why the hell not? Angela had nothing better to do. She plumped down on one of the desk chairs and reached into her denim jacket pocket for her cigarettes.

"Mind if I smoke?"

Tucker's green eyes opened wide for an instant; smoking was strictly forbidden in all of Holly Hills, even the downstairs public lounge, the Goldfish Bowl. It was an offense punishable the first time by grounding for a month, the second time by suspension from classes, and the third time by expulsion. But Angela Torres didn't seem to care.

"Go ahead; they're your lungs." Anthea Tuckerman's nose wrinkled slightly in distaste, and she lit a Rigaud scented candle to mask the smell of the smoke.

Angela peeled out an unfiltered Lucky Strike and lit it up, tossing the match into the gold-trimmed saucer under the scented candle. Inhaling deeply, she narrowed her eyes against the smoke and took a long, calculating look at Tucker.

"So what's all this wonderful shit you hear about me?" she challenged abruptly.

Tucker wasn't fazed for an instant. "Apart from your genius at mathematics, not one single thing," she admitted candidly. "I just wanted to meet you, that's all."

"Why?"

"Because you're one of the most interesting people in the school, and so am I. An interesting person is too rare a treasure to waste. I thought we might become friends."

"Friends!" scoffed Angela. "We haven't one damn thing in common. Just take a look at us."

"Precisely. We're exact opposites. That's what should make our friendship all the more interesting, wouldn't you say?" drawled Tucker, amused.

"Run that by me again," said Angela. "You want me to do your math homework, right?"

"Wrong. I couldn't care less about my math homework. Or any of my homework for that matter. I'm already enrolled at Lyndenwald College; my mother went there before me and her mother before her and so on back for five generations. It's a *fait accompli*, my name was registered the day I was born. Besides, I'm very, very intelligent and my grades are excellent, even in math."

"Okay, then you can do my English homework," countered Angela.

"I'll help you with it, gladly, if you want me to."

"I don't get this," said Angela suspiciously, grinding her cigarette out in the lovely porcelain saucer. "You're a snob from Whipped Cream City and I'm a Puerto Rican from the Bronx. What the hell do you want from me?"

Anthea Tuckerman stood up. "Well, for one thing, I like your style. And I *love* your looks; they're in perfect contrast to my own. Come over here to the mirror. Stand next to me. See what I mean?"

Angela studied their reflections. She saw two girls of equal height and equal beauty—one cool and pale and polished, the other fiery and earthy and wild looking. One dressed like Queen Elizabeth at Balmoral in cashmere and tweed, the other more like Cyndi Lauper, in denims, sneakers, and dozens of bangle bracelets parading up each arm. They were different, all right. In fact, they could not be more dissimilar. But they *did* set each other off. Tucker's pale skin was whiter next to the olive of Angela's face, and Angela's hair and eyes looked even more vivid and glossy when compared with Anthea Tuckerman's. In fact, they looked great together.

"We'll be dynamite going to hops and mixers arm in arm," purred Tucker. "The men will fall off their feet when they see us." Tucker always referred to boys as *men*. It was one of the things boys adored about her. Of course, men or boys, it made no difference, really. Anthea treated them all like naughty babies.

"Forget that noise!" Angela shook her head firmly. "I don't waste my time on such crap. Besides, I already got a . . . somebody."

"Oh?" The green eyes shot a speculative glance sideways at Angela. "A man from . . . home?" Tucker moved delicately around the word *Bronx* as though it were a dirty word.

"Yeah!" Angela's chin came up belligerently, as though defying Miss White Bread to make something of it.

"But is that a reason to hide in your room on mixer

nights? We do have a lot of fun, and all the girls go even if they're going steady with somebody. Don't you like to dance?''

Without knowing it, Tucker had hit a nerve. Next to math and Sam and her baby sister, Angela Torres loved dancing most in the world. She was very good at it and missed it sorely.

Also, Sam hadn't turned up as often at Holly Hills as Angela had expected. He was uncomfortable at the whole complicated process of taking Angela out—signing the book, telling the dorm mistress where they were going, having her back by eleven on the dot. All these rules just made him crazy. Besides, they had no place to be alone together, not so far from home, and the physical frustration made Sam even crazier and left both of them unhappy. All they ever seemed to do on his visits was ride around on the Kawasaki and argue with each other. Angela kept refusing to go to a motel with him; as intimate as they were, she was still not ready to go all the way.

When she had arrived at Holly Hills on her jaunty little Hondo Aero, her first nasty surprise had been . . . no wheels.

"I'm afraid," Miss Appleyard had told her gently, "that only bicycles are permitted here, and a motor scooter doesn't come under the classification of *bicycle*. You'll have to garage it, dear, or else send it back home. Don't worry; it will be perfectly safe with us here, and we'll certainly let you have it back when you go home for the holidays. But we don't allow our girls to drive cars or motorcycles at Holly Hills."

"But it's only a scooter—" Angela had protested. The Apple had shaken her head firmly.

And that had been that. The first thing Angela Torres held against Holly Hills was the loss of her mobility. The school had deprived her of the sense of freedom that her little scooter gave her. There were other grudges too, but that was the first one, and so far the worst one. Except for Sam.

The first time Sam had driven up to Holly Hills to take

Angela out had been a frustrating and impossible situation for both of them.

Accustomed to their freedom, they'd found it unbearable to sign out for only four hours together, putting down in black and white just where they intended to spend their evening.

"That's bogus, man!" Sam exploded as soon as they were outside the school gates. "Bogus jive! Ain't nobody gonna tell me where to go and when to come back!"

"Not you, Sam, me. I'm the one they keep locked up. And I suppose you have to look at it from their point of view. The school is responsible for me now, just like parents. They have to know where I am every minute, in case anything happens."

"Sweetheart, you know I'm not gonna let anything happen to you." Wrapping his arms tightly around her, Sam pulled her close and buried his face in her hair. "Mmm, I've missed you, baby." His breath was warm, and the smell of his leather jacket was so familiar and dear that Angela felt a lump rising in her throat.

"Not here," she whispered, pushing him away. Other girls and boys, leaving the dorm on dates, were staring at Sam and Angela openly, and she felt embarrassment for the first time.

"Where then?" he demanded.

"I . . . I don't know," she confessed. "I don't know where we ought to go. What did you put down? That we were going to a movie? Then I guess we have to go see one. Unless you want to go dancing. Otherwise, I guess we could ride around on your bike."

"It's cold out, baby. Can't we go where it's warm? Just the two of us?" His lips nibbled her neck and earlobes. She felt heat rising through her, spreading from her neck to the rest of her body. Nevertheless, she fought him off.

"I can't, Sam, I just can't! I have to be back by eleven. Let's just go to that movie, okay?"

He regarded her angrily through narrowed eyes. "What the hell goes on here? I thought you were my girl. You been goin' out with anybody else?"

"No, I'm still your girl, Sam. There's nobody else. I just don't want to get kicked out, is all."

How could she explain? That she was lonely here, of no consequence to anybody, that she missed him dreadfully. That she hated the school, feeling cooped up and stifled and resentful of her loss of freedom. Yet even with all that, she wanted desperately to stay at Holly Hills. This school, its repressive rules notwithstanding, was the key to the door of her future. For Angela, it was the way out of shabby semipoverty into limitless possibilities, which she was determined to explore. She sensed that what Holly Hills had to offer was far more valuable than what it temporarily took away.

They saw a film, but neither of them enjoyed it. Even sitting in the dark side by side they were far apart from each other. Usually, they ate movies up like peanuts, gobbling them down happily, washing them down with kisses during scenes that weren't worth watching. But tonight, Sam didn't even put his arm around the back of Angela's seat.

A 124-mile drive to get there, another 124-mile drive to get back, and all for less physical contact than they'd had when Angela was still fourteen years old! No wonder Sam was pissed off.

"I'm not comin' back in such a big hurry, I can tell you, *niña*," he said angrily, as he dropped her outside Laurel Dorm at five minutes to eleven.

"Sam, please . . ." she begged, unwilling to let him go. He was more than just Sam, just her boyfriend; he also represented home to her. To lose him would be to lose everything that was familiar and beloved; it would leave her alone in a world of strangers.

Wordlessly, he snatched her back into his arms for a long, deep kiss, and Angela didn't care who was looking at them as she clutched Sam close.

"I'll see you soon," he promised her.

"Will you, Sam?" Angela had begged eagerly.

"Sure."

But he hadn't. He'd come to see her less and less

frequently. She hadn't seen him in weeks. No wonder she was lonely and listened with half an ear to Tucker's suggestions.

For Anthea Tuckerman had mentioned dancing, and Angela did love to dance. Angela Torres was born to boogie, and she moved to the beat as though she and the music were one.

"Look, this Friday we're mixing with Cumberland, and my brother Pepper goes there. He's a junior, and *very* big in his class. I'll make sure he turns the whole junior class out for the mixer, so you can take your pick. What do you say?" Tucker could be very persuasive when she turned on the charm. The green of her eyes turned from opaque to a kind of gleaming translucence.

It would have taken a much stronger girl than even Angela Torres not to be sorely tempted.

"I haven't got anything to wear," she admitted at last, a confession painfully pulled from her. She wasn't exactly ashamed of her poverty, but she wasn't exactly proud of it, either. Although she had pretended not to notice, Angela was well aware that she looked very different from the rest of Holly Hills and that the few clothes in her wardrobe were not only shabby but out of place. She just wasn't in the same class with the others.

"That's no problem, I'll lend you something of mine. We're the same size."

"But not the same style, you said so yourself."

"Leave it to me, we'll both be knockouts, belles of the ball. What do you say, Angela? Friends?" Anthea Tuckerman held out a smooth perfect right hand.

Angela Torres hesitated. A little voice deep inside her was telling her to be on her guard, to watch out. But she was lonely and isolated, and here was a chance too good to pass up. What was one dance? After all, if she didn't like it, she could always cut out, right?

Taking Tucker's hand in hers, Angela gave it a rough shake. "Friends," she agreed cautiously, in a half growl. The little voice inside her still cried a warning, but Angela ignored it.

CHAPTER FIVE

Making Friends

The next few days flew by. Tucker was the first friend Angela had made at Holly Hills, and she was a valuable one. She appeared to have unlimited resources—money, clothing, even boys, or "men." One out of every two telephone calls into Laurel Dorm was for Tucker. On three school nights a week, the girls were allowed to receive "callers" — dates, really — downstairs in the public lounges, which the girls of Holly Hills and every prep-school boy in Connecticut called the Goldfish Bowl.

It seemed that half the population of the neighboring boys' schools came calling on Anthea Tuckerman. She received every one of them graciously, but one got the impression—the correct impression—that she had screened them all carefully in advance. They were always boys who were leaders—team captains, class presidents, editors of the school paper and the school yearbook, or boys who came from wealthy and powerful families. Tucker always seemed to know what their fathers did, and their fathers always did something influential and very, very profitable.

Tucker had a way of studying people, as if to extract from them whatever they had to offer. Oddly enough, Ismail Figueroa was like her in that respect. Sam too studied people, picking up a turn of phrase here, a mannerism there, and altering it to suit his own personality.

"Take the best and leave the rest," Sam's philosophy, also fitted Tucker Tuckerman's outlook on life.

Anthea Tuckerman was different from any girl Angela

had ever met. She had supreme confidence in herself; she never blushed and she never, never giggled. Just as Angela Torres had been the center of attention back in her intermediate school in the Bronx, so Tucker was the focus of a group of worshipful girls.

Angela despised them all as a group of hypocritical, two-faced, self-seeking ass-lickers. But she felt sorry for them too, because these girls evidently thought so little of themselves that they had surrendered their independence to follow Anthea Tuckerman around, copying her clothes, her speech patterns, and above all, her mannerisms. Angela thought they looked and sounded like clones of Tucker, but without the personality or class.

More than the others, Jennifer Ripley, Missy Farina, and Stacey Underhill earned Angela's deepest contempt, because she could feel the jealous vibes radiating from them, poison arrows aimed straight at her, hating her because Tucker had singled Angela out. Yet they had to be polite to her, even enthusiastic, or Tucker would get angry. Angela couldn't understand their behavior; when *she* disliked somebody, she stayed out of his or her face, or she told him straight where to get off. This hypocrisy on the part of Tucker Tuckerman's clique got on Angela's nerves.

Angela was certain they talked about her behind her back, and she had the uneasy feeling that they knew something about her, some of her secrets. But . . . no, how could that be? That information was locked up in a file cabinet, and she had both Miss Appleyard's and Mrs. Deegan's words of honor that nobody else at Holly Hills would ever know Angela's secret.

In only a day or two, the news that Anthea Tuckerman had taken up Angela Torres spread around the school like wildfire. This was the year that Scottish plaid swept the fashion industry, and little Amanda Cohen, always the leader in designer duds, had been scurrying to and from classes dressed like a bagpipe player. She had even taken to wearing Bonnie Doon knee socks of *two* different plaids at the same time. But no more than an hour after she heard that Anthea Tuckerman had said Angela Torres had style,

Amanda buried her plaids in the bottom of her bottomless closet and emerged on campus wearing a denim jacket with the sleeves rolled up, a printed rayon skirt, dozens of bangle bracelets rattling on her skinny arms, and a genuine pair of beat-up boy's high-top sneakers on her size-five feet. Where she'd gotten the sneakers, nobody knew, but then Amanda always kept her fashion sources jealously guarded.

Suddenly, Angela Torres seemed to have set a new style for Holly Hills. The "South Bronx look" became the latest rage, and it made Angela acutely uncomfortable to see expensive imitations of herself coming and going. When she wore stirrup pants with ankle socks tucked into high-heeled shoes and a large shawl knotted like a sarong over one hip, half the sophomores and most of the freshmen followed suit. Thank heaven the "Angela" fad lasted no more than a month. The rattle of everybody's bangles in class was beginning to drive the teachers to the edge and over it, and there was talk in the Apple's office of banning bracelets entirely from Holly Hills.

After the initial culture shock had worn off, Angela found Tucker fun to be with. She was sharp and witty and those lazy green eyes missed nothing. She was a fund of information about everything that went on at Holly Hills, and Angela was surprised to find herself wanting to hear more. A week ago, she was totally indifferent to her surroundings. Now she asked a million questions about the school and the teachers. Tucker had answers for all of them.

They spent just about every minute of their free time together, mostly in Tucker's room, because out of doors a week-long October rain was falling heavily, turning the campus into a sea of mud. Tucker's room was always warm and bright and cheerful. Of course, Tucker had a roommate, Lolly Madison, but Lolly was working hard on her paper on Lord Byron and starring in the class play, so she was usually in the library or at rehearsals. The two girls often had the room to themselves.

For the first time, Angela felt a stab of dissatisfaction whenever she had to return to her own tiny quarters and look at her ink-stained blob of a roomie. Angela would fantasize that *she* was Tucker's roommate and the wonderful large room was hers too. She barely had a word to say to Sara Grundfest anymore, and never took notice of the pain she was causing.

Sara's pain was very real, but she kept it well hidden. At the core of it was disappointment in Angela, that so independent a girl had so readily allowed herself to be co-opted by the most snobbish girl at Holly Hills without seeing the dangers involved in such a relationship. Sara believed that Angela was heading for some serious heartbreak. Most of all, she didn't want to see Angela Torres turning into another of Anthea Tuckerman's clones.

Yet who could blame Angela? For the first time, others were making a big fuss over her. At home, she had been the second youngest in a large family, so nobody had much time for her, and she was expected to look after her baby sister, whom she adored. In school she had been important, true, but she'd had to be tough to maintain that importance.

Here at Holly Hills, influence had been handed to her on a plate by Anthea Tuckerman. Here she was called "stunning" and "exotic" and fawned over by Tucker's little group of sycophants. It never occurred to Angela that all the commotion she was causing was devoted to her looks rather than her true self, or that Tucker's "friendship" might be a passing thing.

There were things about Tucker that made Angela uncomfortable—her evident snobbery, the malicious way she enjoyed all the brownnosing that went on around her, her contempt for anybody who didn't meet her standards. But she had good qualities too. She was blunt and straightforward and disdainful of lying, like Angela herself. She was vain of her appearance, and with good reason, but she was also impatient with fussing. Anthea Tuckerman's beauty secrets were soap and water, a daily shampoo,

minimal makeup, and lots of hairbrushing. She could be
dressed and ready to go out in the time it took Amanda
Cohen to decide which outfit to wear.

Without thinking about it much, Angela began to wash
her hair every day and make some effort to restrain its wild
quality. She toned down her makeup, using only a little
blusher and mascara. She watched Tucker carefully,
noting her exquisite table manners, her poise, and the fact
that Tucker never seemed to feel the need to raise her
voice. What others did with a shout, Tucker could accom-
plish by a murmur. This was all new to Angela; everybody
back home on Anderson Avenue yelled. They yelled out of
windows, from one room to another, across streets, across
school yards. It had never occurred to Angela before this
that her own voice was too loud, but now she made a
conscious effort to bring down its volume and tone.

"How'd you like a date tonight?" drawled Tucker one
evening.

Angela's eyes opened wide in surprise. "It's
Wednesday," she pointed out.

"True, but one of the Cumberland Prep juniors is
calling on me here this evening, and he could easily bring
along a friend for you."

"What . . . what would I do with a date? I mean, what
would we . . . t-talk about?" Angela felt like a retard
stammering, and she knew her questions were idiotic. But
the palms of her hands had suddenly gone sweaty and cold.

As usual, the two of them were in Tucker's room, but
today they had been studying quietly together, Tucker
making notes for a history paper, Angela working on a
fiendish problem that Professor Woodstein had set her; it
was far more challenging and complex than it had first
appeared to be.

Tucker's sudden invitation had caught her completely
off guard.

"Really, my dear Angela, there's nothing to it." Tucker
smiled. "I mean, that's the whole point of it, isn't it? To
see that nothing dastardly happens to our sacred
virginities. It's not as though we were allowed out, you see.

We just have to sit down there in that shabby room where thousands of nervous girls have sat before us, making intolerable chitchat and praying that we are not overheard. It's a tedious business at best."

"I don't get it!" cried Angela, mystified. "You don't want to do it, yet you do it about three times every week, and now you want to rope me in and drag me along to make more 'intolerable chitchat.' What the hell for?"

"It's a social obligation, don't you see? One simply *must* have some way of meeting eligibles. Besides, it breaks the monotony. What else would you rather do? Sit upstairs and veg out on 'Dynasty'?"

Angela shrugged. "What *this* one simply must do is crack a few books open. My grades aren't hot shit like yours. And I *am* on scholarship. Besides, your 'eligibles' are hardly *my* eligibles, you have to admit. Why don't you get one of the Three Stooges to double-date with you?"

The Three Stooges was Angela's nickname for Stacey Underhill, Missy Farina, and Jennifer Ripley. Tucker thought it an amusing one.

"Because they're so eager they practically drool when they see a man. It's most uncouth. At least you can be relied upon to stay cool. Come on, it'll be fun, and good practice."

"Sitting around in the Goldfish Bowl and acting phony with some stranger in a blazer is not my idea of fun," Angela retorted tartly.

"Then what *is* your idea of fun?"

"Riding my little Honda is fun. Dancing is fun. Movies are fun. Being with Sam Figueroa is fun. And believe it or not, differential calculus is fun."

Tucker's aristocratic nose wrinkled expressively. "You're weird, you know that? Truly, awesomely weird."

"Weird but wonderful." Angela grinned.

"Look, do it for me, all right? Consider it a personal favor. Just come downstairs tonight and let yourself be introduced. Make some polite conversation and let's see how it goes. If you're bored out of your gourd, we'll never do it again, I swear."

Angela shot a yearning glance at her math notebook, with its tantalizing prime-numbers problem, the solution to which was due by her next tutorial. "Have you got anybody special in mind or do I take whatever comes up from the barrel?"

"Leave that to me, pally. I promise you won't be unpleasantly surprised."

"What should I wear?" Angela looked doubtfully down at her old rayon skirt and her sneakers.

"How about this?" A red silk shirt came flying through the air and landed on her face. "And this?" followed by a pale pink cashmere sweater, which draped itself warmly over Angela's curly hair.

"Hey! Get back, Jack!" An angry Angela scrambled to her feet. "I don't want your old clothes, man! I'm no welfare case!"

"Who said anything about charity?" Tucker's jade-colored eyes went wide with surprise. "And those are *not* old clothes; they are some of my favorites. I want them back, and in perfect condition, please. My heavens, didn't you ever have sisters to scrounge things from? I know *I* did, and it's done all the time here. Why, Jennifer Ripley borrowed my tartan skirt three weeks ago! Which reminds me, its return is overdue."

Angela laughed ruefully, shaking her head. "My sisters are much older than I am, but you're right. They wore each other's things all the time. I spoke too soon and too loud. Okay. Thanks, I'll be careful with them. But what do I want a blouse *and* a sweater for?"

"Tuck the red blouse tightly into your jeans, and tie the pink sweater around your shoulders . . . so. See the effect?"

Angela saw. Tucker was right, of course. It was casual, appropriate, yet definitely . . .

She couldn't find the right word, her mind shying away from *sexy*.

Grabbing up her books, Angela headed for the door. "I'd better shower. When is showtime?"

"They'll be here at eight, so please be ready on time.

And for heaven's sake, Angela," she called after Angela's retreating back.

"What?"

"Lose those sneakers!"

At 8:05, the lobby monitor's voice yelled up the stairs. "Tuckerman and Torres! Company!"

Angela flashed a look of panic at Tucker.

"Take it easy," Tucker soothed. "All you have to keep in mind is that these men aren't the real thing, they're just a target of opportunity. This is an exercise in the obligatory mating ritual; it's only practice, so don't worry. Besides, you look knockout."

It was true. Angela Torres looked knockout. She wore thin, strappy sandals with very high heels, so that her long legs appeared to be even longer. The red blouse and the tight jeans did remarkable things for her body, but the pink sweater tied around her shoulders hid some of it, saying "Back off, mister. It's not going to be easy."

Angela had never worn silk or cashmere before, and the textures of the materials were so soft she wanted to keep her face buried in them. The red and pink made her olive skin glow, and Tucker had pulled her abundant hair back from her face and tied it in a matching red ribbon, allowing a few curls to escape onto Angela's forehead. The effect, of wildness tamed, was stunning.

Needless to say, Tucker Tuckerman herself was no Minnie Mouse. She had put on a tweed jacket of absolutely no color at all, as though it were woven of heather grown in a mist, flecked with little bits of pale moss green to match her eyes. The jacket was worn over a camelhair skirt, dark gray wool knee socks and lizardskin loafers. She looked as though she had been born into those clothes, as no doubt she had.

The walk down the stairs was one of the longest Angela had ever taken. At the bottom stood two boys, smiling up at them. They might have been Tweedle Dum and Tweedle Dee. In the first moment of laying eyes on them, Angela thought she was seeing double. In the next moment, she felt as though she might have wandered into the Twilight Zone. In the third moment, she thought, Dios mio, I'll never be able to tell them apart. It's true, all *Yanguis* look alike to us. Both were tall, both thin to the point of scrawniness because they were still growing. Both parted their hair on the same side, both had serious, studious faces, both wore horn-rimmed glasses, the same school crest on their blazers, the same gray flannel trousers, identical L. L. Bean penny loafers. Angela wondered for a split second whether they might be wearing identical jockey shorts, but stifled the giggle that rose to her lips.

But it wasn't as bad as it seemed at first. They had names. One was Anthony Sumner, and he turned out to be Tucker's date. The other, Lindsay Hagen, was evidently intended for Angela, and was smiling at her in open admiration as they bought sodas from the machine, found a corner for four in the Goldfish Bowl, and sat themselves down.

"Please call me Lin. May I call you Angie?"

"No!" Then, realizing she'd overreacted, she softened her voice. "I mean, nobody ever calls me anything but Angela."

"And boy, is that the wrong name for her." Tucker laughed. "She's no angel!"

The crack seemed to break the ice; they all laughed and soon were talking among themselves more naturally. Tony, Tucker's date, was preparing for Yale and a career in political science, and Lin was a classics major, carrying twelve credits in Latin and Greek this semester.

"A classics major!" Tucker's winglike eyebrow shot up in astonishment. "I didn't think there were any of those left on the planet. I presumed you were all extinct!"

Lin smiled shyly; he was really rather sweet, thought Angela, but too subdued and colorless for her. She liked a man with glitz and power. She liked . . . Sam.

"Oh, there are a few of us left, living in caves, trying to invent fire, gnawing on dinosaur bones to survive."

"My roommate is a classics major," put in Angela.

Tucker shrugged one slim shoulder disdainfully. "Oh,

your roommate!'' Having dismissed poor Sara Grundfest with a mere four syllables, she turned to Lin again. "But what can a classics major *do*?" she wanted to know.

That shy smile again. "We teach, of course. The lucky ones publish something, and the very lucky ones get to go out on an archaeological dig.''

"Now *that* sounds interesting." Tucker smiled up into Lindsay's face. "Will you be one of the very lucky ones?''

"I hope so." He turned away from Tucker to talk to Angela. "What are you studying?''

"As little as I can get away with." Angela laughed. "But my main interest is in mathematics.''

"Haven't you heard?" drawled Tucker. "Angela is our resident math genius. We're all very proud of her.'' Was she kidding or what?

"Math!" Tony's face screwed up in horror. "My Achilles' heel! I could never add two and two.''

"Then politics is totally the ideal profession for you,'' drawled Tucker, and everybody laughed again. She certainly knew how to keep the conversational ball rolling —with zingers. Her wit was terrific, when it wasn't aimed at you.

"What are you planning to do with your life?" Lin asked Angela quietly.

It was a question that always threw her, because she was afraid people would laugh at the answer. So far, she pretended that she hadn't made up her mind. Even Sam didn't know of her intentions. But Lin was so serious-minded, so sweet, that Angela felt somehow certain he wouldn't laugh.

"I'd like to study astrophysics, and go into some form of space technology.''

Tucker overheard them and burst out laughing. "You mean like Sally Ride," she teased, putting one manicured finger exactly on the spot.

It was true. Angela Torres *did* want to be another Sally Ride; she yearned to journey out into space, to learn everything she could about what was out there in the stars. Space technology fascinated her.

"Even though seven people died in the Challenger? Including two women?" he asked.

Angela lifted her chin and her dark eyes flashed. "I'm not afraid."

Lin returned her look warmly. "Good for you. Isn't it ironic," said Lin softly. "I want to journey inside the earth to discover the old, and you want to journey off the earth to discover the new."

But Tucker was getting bored with this conversation because it wasn't about her. Clapping her long white hands together to gain everybody's attention, she started talking about the latest "in" movie—an Australian film that Angela had never heard of and certainly hadn't seen.

Left out, Angela subsided into silence and looked around her. The Laurel Dorm bowl was full of goldfish tonight; freshman, sophomore, and junior Holly Hills girls, dressed casually but with care and a little makeup, sharing sofas with or sitting in chairs across from tall boys, short boys, plump boys, thin boys, boys with and without facial blemishes, boys whose voices had changed, and boys whose voices still made embarrassing squeaks at the wrong times. The name of the game was "popularity," but it seemed to Angela that sometimes the rules were too tough and that the stakes weren't high enough.

There was so much striving in the room, you could feel the pressure. Pressure to be liked, to find somebody special, pressure to *make* something happen instead of letting it take its own sweet time in its own sweet way.

Whew! This was too heavy for Angela. Thank heaven for Sam, she thought, then felt a stab of irritation that he hadn't been to see her in weeks, that it wasn't Sam sitting here in the bowl instead of these two not very memorable boys from some Velveeta school whose name she'd already forgotten.

But then she couldn't expect Sam or anybody else in his right mind to drive one hundred and twenty four miles up and one hundred and twenty four miles back just to sit in the Goldfish Bowl and drink Pepsi.

So what was Angela to do? How do you have a little fun around here without a date, especially when the dates themselves weren't so much fun?

"Well?" demanded Tucker Tuckerman when the boys had finally headed reluctantly back to school for curfew and she and Angela had gone upstairs.

Angela shrugged. "I've had worse times at the dentist," she admitted. "But are all the boys you know so . . . so . . . bland?"

"I suppose if it's chili peppers you're used to, then, yes, I suppose most of them are," conceded Tucker. "But hang in there until Friday night when we go to the mixer. If you like something sweet, there's a gift-wrapped assortment to choose from—maybe you'll get a nougat instead of a nut."

Angela grinned in spite of herself. Tucker really had a way with words. "All right, I'll give it a try. But I'm warning you, *muchacha,* if I don't like it I'm cutting right out."

"Oh, you'll like it," Tucker assured her confidently. "Just wait until you see how we part the waters. You'll have a great time, that I can personally guarantee."

"Yeah, well, we'll see." But inside, Angela felt a stab of apprehension. She had no idea what she might be letting herself in for.

CHAPTER SIX

Belle of the Ball

Tucker Tuckerman was, as always, right on the money. The two of them *did* part the waters when they came into the dance arm in arm, Tucker in pale green, Angela in red and pink, the ice princess and the gypsy.

You could hear the gasps of surprise from the rest of the Holly Hills sophomores. The Cumberland Prep boys uttered low whistles and came lumbering over like puppies yelping for Alpo. Within minutes, both Tucker and Angela were surrounded by a pack of Cumberland juniors, a sea of eager male faces, an explosion of clamoring male voices.

"Hi, my name is—" they said to Angela.

"Hello, there, I'm Robert, I'm Josh, I'm Don, I'm Tommy, I'm Alistair (*Alistair?*), I'm Willie, I'm Woody, I'm Thumper and let me show you why they call me that—" they panted at Angela.

"Who are *you*?" they asked Angela. "Why haven't we ever seen *you* before?"

"You're beautiful," said one voice to Angela abruptly, without ceremony. "Let's dance."

Angela looked for the voice's owner. Not very tall and built on the stocky side, his Cumberland blazer stretching tightly across his shoulders and chest but hanging loosely over his torso, evidence of a strong upper body and a thin waist. With light blue eyes shining out of a deeply tanned face, hair somewhere between light brown and reddish gold bleached by the sun, he was, all in all, not too shabby.

She cocked one eyebrow at him, a challenge. "*Can* you dance?"

"Try me. I think you won't go away disappointed."

And off they went, leaving the crowd of boys looking after her with hunger in their eyes. Some of them drifted away to find other girls, but many of them stayed behind to worship at Anthea Tuckerman's shrine. Soon, some lucky and deserving preppie had carried off the prize, proudly leading Tucker out onto the dance floor, where she insisted that they dance near Angela and her partner.

This boy might not be a Sam Figueroa where dancing was concerned, but he had a few pretty good moves.

"Yeah, you're an okay dancer," admitted Angela grudgingly, but her eyes were shining with enjoyment as she moved tightly to the music. "What's your name? I hope you're not the Alistair."

The boy uttered a loud laugh. "Michael Andrew Elliott Harrison, but call me Mickey, everybody does. And you?"

"And me what?"

"Even the most beautiful of Grecian vases has a handle. What's yours?"

"Angela Torres," she threw over her shoulder as she spun around him.

"Angela. Angel. It fits."

"Yeah? Tucker Tuckerman says it's the wrong name for me."

"Tucker Tuckerman should have her eyes examined."

"I heard that, Mickey," accused Tucker, who was dancing only inches away. "There's nothing wrong with my eyes."

"Amen to that." The sweaty preppie she was dancing with sighed. He was already hopelessly in love with Anthea Tuckerman, caught like a fly in her web.

When the music changed to a slow dance, Angela suddenly found herself wrapped in Mickey Harrison's arms. It felt surprisingly good. In her nostrils was his masculine scent, composed of shaving lotion and freshly laundered shirt, wool blazer and boy's sweat; it was far from unpleasant. Mickey held her firmly but not pressed too close to his body. The chaperons at the Holly Hills mixers were strict as well as eagle-eyed and would publicly reprimand any couple they saw nuzzling on the dance floor.

Mickey didn't talk much, and that was something of a relief. Accustomed all her life to the rapid rhythms of the Spanish language, she found the lazy drawls, clipped tones, and imitation Ivy League lockjaw of so many Holly Hills girls painful to her ears. She even found welcome, by contrast, the upper-class Spanish of the two snobbish Castilian girls. Now that Tucker Tuckerman had made Angela Torres the latest rage, Amelia and Mercedes had come hastily around to mend their social fences.

Content just to dance, to follow Mickey Harrison's lead, Angela drifted across the floor, allowing her mind to wander. Oddly enough, it wandered not to Mickey, not even to Sam, but to the murderous math problem. A brand-new approach struck her suddenly, something that she hadn't tried before, something that just might work. Now, if she could only remember it until she got back to her books . . .

"Cutting in," drawled a new voice, and Angela was startled out of her reverie by the sudden appearance of a tall boy, demanding to dance.

Reluctantly, Mickey handed her over. "I'll be back, Angel," he told her in a low tone as the new boy danced her off.

What the hell is this? thought Angela indignantly. What am I, some kind of package to be delivered by UPS?

Shooting an angry look up at the interloper, Angela missed a step in surprise. She was dancing with Tucker!

No, it wasn't Tucker, yet here were the same cat-green eyes, thin high-arched nose, arrogant full mouth, the same pale blond hair, the same tall slender body, but male, all male.

"Hey, I bet I know who you are! You're Pepper Tuckerman, right? You couldn't be anybody but Tucker's twin brother."

"I have that dubious distinction," he teased, with a tone and inflection exactly like his sister's. It was eerie, how much they resembled each other. "And you, of course, couldn't be anybody but Angela Torres."

"I have that dubious distinction," she mocked him solemnly.

"My sister has told me all about you." He smiled.

"All?" Angela pretended alarm, widening her dark eyes until they were enormous, but she felt an uneasy stab of genuine alarm at the back of her mind. Did anybody here know *all* about her? Apart from Miss Appleyard, of course.

"She told me that you're different and interesting and a whiz at mathematics. The first two I can see for myself. The last I accept on faith."

"Well, keep the faith, brother," cracked Angela, relieved.

Pepper Tuckerman threw his golden head back and laughed loud and long. "You're terrific!"

"Cutting in," insisted a determined voice, and the next thing Angela knew, Michael Harrison was dancing her away again.

"Hey, what the hell is this all about?" demanded Angela. "I feel like I'm in some kind of revolving door!"

"Cutting in is traditional at dances like these. You should accept it as a compliment. It only means that you're popular and desirable," Mickey assured her.

"Well, I feel more like a bowl of rice and beans being handed around the dinner table," grumbled Angela. "Everybody gets to take a spoonful before I'm passed on to the next."

"No more spoonfuls," said Mickey firmly. "We're sitting out." Taking her hand, he led Angela off the floor to a corner of the room where chairs and small tables stood near the refreshment stand, and there he sat her down. "Would you like some punch?"

Angela's face screwed up in a grimace of disgust. "I tasted that stuff, and I'd rather eat a pillow. Don't they have any Diet Coke or Pepsi Light? I'll even take a club soda or a ginger ale."

"I'll rustle some up from the machine. Do I have to strap you down or will you stay put in this chair?" he asked her pleadingly.

Angela shrugged. "Hey, you knew the job was dangerous when you took it."

"Okay, I'll go, but I'll hate every minute of it." And Mickey vanished, pushing his way through the dancers.

As if by magic, a crowd of boys instantly appeared from nowhere to grab the chairs near Angela, competing loudly for her attention. Laughing, she looked from one eager face to the next, ignoring their pleadings but enjoying the stir she was causing. This was all new to her. She had never before been literally "the belle of the ball," and she was having a wonderful time, just as Tucker had promised.

"Shoo! Scat! Take a hike, you turkeys! This lady is taken!" Pepper Tuckerman loomed up suddenly, and the others scattered at his command. Evidently, Pepper threw as much weight around Cumberland Prep as Tucker did at Holly Hills.

"Hey, man, who told you I was taken?" demanded Angela, not too pleased about losing her crowd of admirers.

"My heart told me. *Mi corazón,*" and he looked at her so appealingly that she had to smile back. His eyes certainly were green, and they glowed. He was one foxy *muchacho,* and he knew it.

Sliding gracefully into the seat beside her, Pepper reached for Angela's hand. But what he came up with was empty air.

"Back off, cowboy! Where do you get off putting the moves on me? I don't remember issuing you any invitations."

Pepper grinned, leaning very close to Angela so he could be heard over the music. "Sweetness, you're one party I'd like to crash."

Angela couldn't help but laugh out loud. "You're exactly like your sister, you know that?"

"Thanks," he answered dryly. "I don't know whether to kiss you or kill you for that one. But I'd be more than happy to demonstrate the differences between me and Tuck. At your earliest convenience. Shall we set a date?"

"Say, how did you ever get a name like Pepper?" asked Angela curiously. "And how come you're both the same age, but you're a junior, while she's only a soph?"

Pepper Tuckerman threw out his hands. "Questions, questions! One at a time, please. Okay. I don't tell this to everybody, but I'm making an exception in your case, and I expect you to return the favor some day. We had a Dutch ancestor who came over here in the 1600s and acquired roughly two-thirds of upstate New York. Naturally, the family is still very grateful, so generations of Tuckermans were named after him. In my generation, I was it. You see before you Piers-Paul Tuckerman. They tell me that in my adorable toddler days I could pronounce only 'Pepper,' and Pepper I remained. Boring, right?"

"Right." Angela grinned.

"Then you'll find this even more tedious. I'm a year ahead of her in school because I did summer school for three years in a row. Why, you ask?"

"No, I don't."

"Then I'll tell you. I'm impatient, little Angela. Competitive and impatient. I want to be out there in the great, big world, doing great big things. Not for me basketball camp in July and soccer camp in August. Tennis is a waste of my precious time, and so is squash, although I'm good at both and I'll pick up a racquet if it's socially useful. I like to swim, but I can do that all year round, because we have an indoor pool at home. What I *can't* do is get back a minute of wasted time. So I'll be graduating a year before Ms. Anthea Tuckerman, and I intend to stay at least a year ahead of her our whole lives long. You think it's easy being born a twin?"

Before Angela could answer, she saw Michael Harrison

come walking toward them, carrying two cans of soda. His face, when he saw Pepper, lost its smile and became somewhat grim about the corners of the mouth. He handed one Coke to Angela.

"Tuckerman," he acknowledged curtly.

"Harrison." Pepper nodded in return.

"If you'll excuse us . . ."

"No, Harrison, *you* excuse *us*!" Pepper stood up, and he and Mickey stood almost toe to toe, glaring at each other.

"*Dios mío!*" yelled Angela furiously, springing up from her chair. "What do you dumb dudes think you're going to do? Cut each other up? You guys are too much, you know that? The pair of you arguing over me like both of you have some *rights*! Like I got nothing to say about it! Like you two are dogs and I'm the bone! Well, listen up! This is a late news bulletin, just in. *Nobody* owns a piece of Angela Torres except Angela Torres!"

And with those exasperated words, she ran off, pushing her way roughly through the dancers to get to the exit, not looking to the right or to the left.

"Angela!" called Tucker Tuckerman after her, as she saw her friend storm past. But Angela didn't see or hear Tucker, she was so indignant and humiliated.

It wasn't until she was safe in her room in Laurel Dorm that she took a deep breath and attempted to get control of herself. Sara Grundfest looked up from her books, astonished, but Angela's scowl told her more eloquently than words that she wasn't receptive to a greeting just now. So Sara wisely kept silent, but her eyes behind their thick lenses grew round with wonder and worry.

Three-quarters of an hour later, Angela, having calmed down and having made good progress with her math problem, suddenly flashed on the ridiculous sight of Pepper and Mickey nose to nose and saw the humor in the situation. When she did, she burst out laughing.

"*Ay, mi madre!* They are all alike, boys! Who would have thought that a couple of Wonder Bread preppies would have the same *machismo* in their souls as Sam Figueroa!''

"Where on earth did you disappear to?" demanded Tucker later. "I looked for you for hours!"

"I came back to the dorm. Look, Tucker, I told you I'd cut out if I wasn't enjoying myself, and I wasn't, so I did."

Having had time to cool out, Angela had the sneaking feeling that she had probably overreacted, that instead of losing her temper she ought to have been flattered. But she couldn't actually admit she was wrong, so her words and tone were defensive.

"I don't understand you, Angela!" cried Tucker, vexed. "You appeared to be having such a good time! And you were so popular! Why, everybody in the Cumberland Prep junior class wanted to be introduced to you! They were all asking me about you. And without even a word to me you took off like an express train. Don't you like men?"

"Of course I like men, what do you suppose? But I think I like them better one at a time, not all of them coming at me at once. It was like a cattle stampede in there."

"You poor thing, I really sympathize," murmured Tucker with sweet sarcasm. "Any one of the Three Stooges would have jumped for joy to be in your predicament, and you run off like Cinderella on the stroke of midnight. I'm surprised you didn't leave a glass sneaker behind. Besides, I thought you and Michael Harrison were hitting it off splendidly. At least it looked as though you were."

"He's okay," replied Angela gruffly and a little evasively. Some street-wise instinct told her not to bring up Tucker's twin brother. Evidently Tucker hadn't seen anything of what went down between Pepper and Mickey, and that was probably for the best.

"I used to date Mickey, oh, ages ago. He's quite sweet. His father is in the Street, you know."

Angela didn't know. "What do you mean, in the street?

Down and out? Tap City? Then how can he afford to send Mickey to Cumberland Prep?''

Tucker laughed, a ripple of silver. "Honestly, Angela, you're priceless. The *Street*! Wall Street! He's a stockbroker. *Very* well-to-do."

Terrific, Angela thought. Score another dumb fumble against Torres, Angela. "He's a nice guy, I suppose, but not exactly my type."

"Your type! What *is* your type?"

Angela's grin was lopsided and wry. "Tuckerman, if you have to ask, then I can't tell you. All I can say is that he's dynamite gorgeous, built, his hair is jet black and he looks like John Travolta, only younger and better."

"Mmmm, sounds like I could go for him myself," purred Tucker. "This must be your Sam Figueroa. When do we get to meet that paragon of masculinity?"

A sigh escaped Angela. "I wish I knew that myself. Sam came up twice, and then just couldn't get it together to come up again. He works and goes to school, and between the two of those things, Connecticut is one helluva long haul for just a date. If only they'd let me have my Honda back and give me some time off during a weekend—"

"At Holly Hills? Are you real? You have to be crazy to even dream about such a thing! You're enrolled in one of the most select, most strictly run girls' schools in America! If you wanted time off, you should have gone to Bronx Science! But possess your soul in patience; when we're seniors, we get a lot more privileges. We don't have to live in Laurel Dorm, and we can go out on the honor system."

"I'll never make it," groaned Angela. "It's a lifetime away."

"Do you love Sam?" Tucker Tuckerman asked curiously.

"Yes . . . no . . . yes. I guess I do. I think I'm too young to worry about 'real love' and 'forever' and bullshit like that, but I haven't seen anybody in all my life who can hold a candle to Sam. He's . . . strong, you know? Like a man, not a boy. He takes responsibility. You think a man

THE WRONG NAME FOR ANGELA   69

has got to be somebody in a school jacket with gold buttons, somebody with a rich father.

"But *my* definition of a man is somebody who takes responsibility for his own life and what he does, who does what he has to, no matter how young or old he is. I've seen boys of forty, and men of fifteen. My own father was working hard at fifteen, taking care of his brothers and sisters. That's a man. That's my definition of a woman too. Right now, we're girls, because our parents and our school are responsible for us. When we can take that responsibility over for ourselves, and do what we have to do, that's when we can call ourselves women."

"Well!" Tucker Tuckerman's eyebrow shot way up. "That's quite a lecture, practically a sermon. I had no idea you were so . . . liberated!"

But at the same time Tucker was speaking to Angela, she was saying silently to herself, "Is that how *you* became a woman, Angela Torres? By taking responsibility for your actions and going to jail? Or did they catch you at it, whatever you did. I wonder what it was you went to jail for. I would really love to find out. I *must* get Jennifer Ripley on the stick. . . ."

CHAPTER SEVEN

Getting into Trouble

Overnight, Angela's life underwent some heavy and incredible changes. Word of her new popularity spread through Cumberland Prep like a brushfire. Even boys at the other schools, like Chalfont and Ames, began to hear about Angela Torres and how she'd wasted Pepper Tuckerman and Mickey Harrison. Suddenly this girl was like Mount Everest—the ultimate challenge for brave men. Now most of the telephone calls that came in to Laurel Dorm were for Angela Torres, calls from boys she didn't even know, inviting her to go out on dates, asking her to let them visit her in the Holly Hills Goldfish Bowl.

Even though Tucker Tuckerman assured her that it was common practice to blind-date, that all the other girls did it (if they were lucky enough to be asked), Angela still couldn't get over sixteen years of South Bronx conditioning. You don't talk to strangers; any stranger is a potential enemy in the streets; you had to be on guard at all times; so she kept saying no.

"Angela? It's Mickey."

"Yeah, what's happening, bro?"

"I hear you've broken half the hearts in Connecticut, just by saying no."

"Then you hear wrong, *muchacho*. Just some dumb-ass schoolboys looking to get lucky. No hearts involved at all."

"Are you going to turn me down too?" asked Mickey Harrison plaintively over the telephone. "I've got a heart, and all it wants is to take you out Saturday night, just a movie and maybe a hamburger. Or a chili dog, if you'd prefer."

"Is that some kind of racist crack?" growled Angela, only half serious. She was actually happy to hear from Mickey, and nobody was more surprised about that than Angela herself. His voice on the phone made her smile.

"Yup. I thought I'd have a Velveeta cheese sandwich on Wonder Bread with Miracle Whip. But I'll treat you to a taco or an enchilada, whatever you prefer."

"We Hispanics all look alike to you, Paco, don't we? As it happens, I'm not Mexican, I'm Puerto Rican. Read my lips. *Pway*-to-*ree*-can. That means I'd be an American citizen even if I hadn't been born in the Bronx, which I was. I'm as Yankee as you are, Ace."

"I wish I were there to read your lips." Mickey sighed, ignoring her indignation. "Not to mention what else I'd like to do to your lips."

"Put it on ice, Slick. I got no eyes for fooling around with you."

"Oh, you've got eyes, Angel, such big, beautiful black eyes . . ." He sighed dramatically.

Angela couldn't help it, she had to laugh. "Well, you all look alike to me too," she admitted. "Especially in those monkey jackets. And I have to admit, I love tacos. *And* enchiladas, and chili, and refried beans, and tostadas, and burritos—"

"Hey, hold on! My pitiful allowance has to last until the end of the month. If I promise not to wear the old school blazer, do you think you'll recognize me about seven-thirty on Saturday night?"

"*Tal vez,* Paco."

"Does that mean yes?"

"It means maybe."

As it happened, she had a great time. Mickey was great fun to be with. He was smart and sunny-tempered, good-looking with a sense of humor. The first thing he did, after he and Angela had signed out and they were on their way into town in his little Nissan, was to apologize.

"I'm very sorry. It gave me a lot to think about, you storming out like that. You were absolutely right, you know. The two of us *were* behaving like dumb-ass jerks. It just never occurred to me to ask you what *you* wanted, and I apologize for my stupidity and insensitivity. But nobody ever put it to me like that before."

"You mean like at the top of her lungs?" Angela smiled. "It's my turn to apologize about that, and I'm sorry. I have a terrible temper. Latinos are famous for their tempers. We're hot-blooded."

"Oh, God, I surely do hope so," moaned Mickey, folding his hands and gazing prayerfully up to heaven.

"Don't get cute. Lay one finger on me and you're dead meat."

"You have a sweet, romantic way of putting things, you know that, Angela?"

And he didn't. Lay one finger on her, that is. Instead, they saw a revival of *Singin' in the Rain,* which Angela adored, after which they went to a popular school hangout where the hamburgers were big and juicy and smothered in onions. They ate a burger apiece, then split a bowl of chili between them. Then, groaning, their bellies about to pop, they drove back to Holly Hills in time for Angela to easily make the Saturday night eleven-o'clock curfew.

Michael Harrison turned to face her as she was getting out of the car, and his face was serious. "I had a super time, Angela. Thank you."

"Me too, Mickey." She smiled. "The movie was *fantastico. Gracías.* "

"Again soon?"

"Tal vez. "

"That means maybe, right?"

Angela started to shrug, then changed her mind. "In this case, it means yes," she answered softly.

It wasn't until she was in her pajamas and brushing her teeth that Angela realized she hadn't thought of Sam all evening. Not even once.

It seemed that all of Laurel Dorm knew that Angela

Torres was going out with Michael Harrison. It began to dawn on her that this was some kind of big deal—after three or four girls had congratulated her on her catch, including Amanda Cohen, who was *very* choosy.

"Why is everybody making so much noise about me and Mickey?" demanded Angela of Tucker, as they carried their trays on the dining-room line.

"Because Mickey Harison is *definitely* an eligible. I ought to know. I went out with him for months."

This took Angela by surprise, the calm way that Tucker could talk about it. "How come you stopped dating him yourself?"

"Oh, we just sort of . . . drifted apart," murmured Tucker. "I met Boots Callaghan, and we began to go steady for a while."

"Yeah? What did *his* father do?" cracked Angela.

She meant it as a joke, yet Anthea Tuckerman took the question not only seriously but as a natural one. "Judge Callaghan is in line for a Supreme Court appointment; everybody knows that."

"And where's Boots today?"

"Harvard."

That seemed to end that conversation; at least, Tucker didn't volunteer any more information, and Angela didn't ask for any. They headed directly for the table that Tucker always considered her own; by now, she had *made* it her own, and no freshman or sophomore girl dared to sit there except by Tucker's express invitation.

As they set down their trays Angela saw Sara Grundfest moving slowly down the room, looking for a place to sit. She raised one arm to wave, but Tucker pulled it down firmly and slammed the two remaining chairs forward against the table, signifying "taken."

"Are you serious?" she hissed at Angela.

"She's my roommate!"

"That's neither your fault nor your responsibility. The fact remains, she is certainly not one of *us*."

"And I *am*?" Angela's eyes widened in surprise.

"Why not, if I say so?"

This was hardly the answer Angela expected, but she found herself choking back the retort that sprang to her lips. Even as Angela wanted to demand of Anthea Tuckerman what gave her the right to decide who was "us" and who wasn't, the words died in her throat. She *wanted* to belong, to be accepted by the elite of the school as "one of us." The sight of little Sara's stricken face when she saw Angela at a "taken" table did nothing to make Angela feel better about it, but at least she had admitted it to herself for the first time. Even if she had choked on the words. She wanted to belong. She wanted to be a "somebody" at Holly Hills. She wanted to stay at Holly Hills.

Angela was digging her popularity, having fun on her dates with Mickey, deepening her friendship with Tucker. These were some of the benefits that Holly Hills had to offer, along with her scholarship. Why not take them and enjoy them to the full? Wasn't she entitled?

With every day that passed, the benefits looked better and better. Angela was really enjoying her status as one of the power centers of the sophomore class. Only now it wasn't little kids she was protecting; these were girls of her own age who flocked around her in admiration, who copied her style and her slang, who flattered her and praised her to her face.

"Help me with this math problem," begged Missy Farina.

"Shoot."

"How many numbers are there between one hundred and one thousand that aren't divisible by two? How many aren't divisible by three? How many aren't divisible by two or three?"

"Four hundred fifty. Five hundred ninety-nine. Three hundred." Angela rattled the numbers off with ease.

"Are you sure?"

"Sure I'm sure. It's just simple arithmetic. Look. There are nine hundred numbers between a hundred and a thousand, right? Half of them are odd and half are even, right? Only the even numbers are divisible by two, and that makes four hundred fifty odd numbers that can't be divided by two. See if you can figure out the rest of the problem, now that you know the answers. If I tell you how to do everything, you'll never learn math.''

"I never *want* to learn math," said Missy with a pout.

"Tough shit, Farina. You'll never make it in life if you don't at least learn to add and subtract. How you gonna know if your credit-card bills are correct?"

"My daddy will pay them until I get married, and after that my husband will pay them. So why should I care?"

"You make me sick, Farina." But you also make me a little jealous, added Angela to herself.

Envy was the other side of the status coin. Every time she went out with Mickey, she had to borrow something to wear from Tucker. For the first time in her life, Angela was feeling stabs of envy—not of what other people *were*, but of what they *had*, something she'd never even cared about before.

Also, her schoolwork was starting to suffer, even her precious mathematics. When she'd had nothing else going for her at Holly Hills, she'd kept her nose to the grindstone and hit the books. But now that she was part of a whole new social life, Angela's priorities shifted, and she began to lose touch with her center.

She missed a computer hour. There were four computers at Holly Hills and a lot of educational software, but the computers were so in demand that they were booked up weeks in advance. People who failed to show up for computer time lost it. To advanced math students especially, computer time was precious, saving long hours of laborious arithmetical calculations, freeing the student for the abstract thinking the problem called for. But Angela's attention was elsewhere, and she simply forgot that she had reserved computer time. It was a serious infringement of the school rules, and she had to pay for it by doing all her calculations on paper. It took hours.

Even worse, for the first time she was late to a tutorial of Professor Woodstein, which showed unheard-of disrespect and rudeness to the world-renowned teacher.

She'd been so busy pawing through Tucker's closet,

trying on Tucker's clothes, that the hours had fled. Before she knew it, the hands of the clock had reached tutorial hour. With a gasp, Angela dropped an expensive argyle sweater in a heap on Tucker's floor and literally flew out the door, racing across the campus on her long legs, her heart pumping with the exertion.

Too late. The tutorial had begun by the time she arrived, out of breath and red in the face from running and embarrassment. Professor Woodstein said nothing but gave Angela a look of mild reproof that went straight to her heart. Sinking meekly down into her seat, she kept her mouth shut for the entire hour, too mortified to raise her hand to ask a question or even to participate in the lively discussion.

They had a special relationship, the old man and the young Puerto Rican girl, a relationship based on mutual respect and a mutual love for the beauty and precision of mathematics. Whenever Angela would visit him in his office, the old teacher would shut the door, light up his pipe, and give her a chance to sneak a forbidden Lucky Strike, under the cover of his pipe smoke. They would puff together happily as they went over Angela's assigned calculus problems.

Now she was letting him down, coming in late, and worse, coming in only half prepared. With less time allotted to study and more time allotted to play, Angela's assignments just never seemed to get done. Thank heaven for Anthea Tuckerman and her little group of merry elves. They divvied up Angela's homework according to who was best at what and knocked it off for her.

Angela knew it was wrong, very wrong. She knew that it would get her in trouble even if it was never found out. How would she pass her midterms? How would she retain her scholarship? She knew she was charting a shaky course through rock-filled waters, but she put it out of her mind as she copied Stacey Underhill's English homework into her notebook in her own handwriting. Time enough to think about it when the time came.

Sara Grundfest watched her with an aching heart, saying

nothing, but her huge eyes were troubled behind her thick glasses. If Angela needed help in her studies, Sara always stood ready to give it. Not to do it for her, but to help her to do it for herself. It pained Sara to watch Angela changing every day, and not for the better.

Where was the old, unique, independent, dashing Angela Torres? She was turning into another one of Tucker Tuckerman's clones, better than the rest maybe, but still dancing to Tucker's tune and still pulled by Tucker's strings. It was criminal, thought Sara mournfully. Criminal and a waste.

"Look, Angela, you know I'm crazy about you," said Mickey earnestly. "Cut me an inch of slack. This is our fifth date, and you've still got me backed into a corner."

Angela turned her face away so that Mickey wouldn't see her lips tremble. She knew what he was driving at. So far, she hadn't even kissed him. He was right, it wasn't fair. He'd been the perfect gentleman, but she hadn't cut him his inch of slack.

And she *wanted* to kiss Mickey Harrison, that was the funny part of it. Angela wasn't sure when or how it had happened, but her simple liking for him had deepened to something . . . different.

When they'd first begun to date, Angela looked on him only as somebody amusing to have a good time with, no threat to her relationship with Sam Figueroa. But as time went by and Sam's telephone calls became shorter in duration and fewer in number, he became shadowy . . . somebody she had to concentrate hard to remember.

On the other hand, Mickey Harrison was here, beside her in his little Nissan, very real, very warm, very attractive. And wanting very badly to kiss her. Not only that, he was an "eligible," a boy that other girls envied her having, a boy worth holding on to.

"Angela, I can't go on like this much longer. Play me or trade me." Mickey's voice was low and passionate.

"I . . . I'm not sure . . ." confessed Angela.

Mickey could scarcely believe his ears. This was the first

time he'd ever heard hesitation in Angela Torres' voice, the first time she had ever expressed uncertainty to him. It was a call to action, and he obeyed.

Reaching for her, he pulled her tightly into his arms and kissed her firmly on the mouth.

At first she resisted, trying to break off the kiss and twist out of his arms. But Mickey's passion was contagious. Very soon, it got to Angela, heating her too, and she yielded with a little moan, pressing her body against his and opening her lips to his probing tongue.

It was crowded in the little car; Angela felt the steering wheel in her ribs as they kissed, and then it didn't matter to her. Once again she tried to protest as she felt Mickey's hands encircling her breasts, but that protest too was soon lost in the magical wonder of the kiss.

Suddenly, her breasts were cold; Mickey had pulled up her sweater and undone her bra. Then they grew warm under his exploring hands and lips.

She knew she should stop him, but she didn't want to. She was caught up in the fire of his hands and mouth. It had been so long, so long since she'd been in Sam's arms, she'd almost forgotten the incredible pleasure. Automatically, her hands reached up and twined themselves in Mickey's red-gold hair, pressing him closer to her. She wanted this to go on forever.

But when she felt his hand on the zipper of her jeans, Angela grabbed Mickey's fingers tightly, pulling them away.

"Ah, let me," he whispered. "Beautiful Angel, let me, please."

"No, no, no, no . . ." Her whisper was hoarse but firm. "No way, Mickey. Not that far that fast—" Her words were cut short by another long, deep kiss. He pressed her back on the seat.

Now Angela felt as though she was on a merry-go-round that was going too swiftly, making her dizzy. She had to get off. *Had to!*

"You're so beautiful, and I want you so much," he begged.

With an enormous effort of will, Angela called a halt. She pushed hard against Mickey until he let her go. Sitting up straight, she pulled her sweater down over her naked breasts, the wool irritating her sensitive nipples.

"*Hombre,* this isn't gonna work." She moved away from him. "I like you a lot, but I'm not ready for anything this heavy. Maybe we shouldn't see each other anymore."

Mickey's face darkened like a raincloud in a summer sky. "Maybe we shouldn't," he agreed shortly, his voice tight and angry. "You just won't give a guy a break, will you? I'll take you back to the school."

Suddenly, something snapped in Angela. The thought of not seeing Mickey became unbearable. She was losing an eligible. It might appear to Holly Hills as though *he'd* dumped *her,* and how would that look to Anthea Tuckerman? Not to mention that Jennifer, Missy, and Stacey would be able to snicker at Angela behind her back. She'd be a loser, when what she wanted was to be a winner. She had never cared for that crap before, but suddenly it was very important that the rest of Holly Hills think Angela Torres was a winner.

"Mickey," she said quietly.

He turned to look at her, and Angela pulled the sweater up and over her head, shivering a little, but reaching for him.

"Ah, baby, you're cold. Let me fix that."

Then his strong arms were tightly around her, his lips were buried in her throat. Angela's eyes closed, but not before one tear had escaped to roll silently down her cheek.

CHAPTER EIGHT

Pepper

"Well, folks, it's mess-up time! I'm going to screw up my midterms," announced Angela angrily to nobody in particular, slamming her textbooks down onto her bed. "There goes my scholarship! God*damn*!"

Nobody in particular looked up in horror from her history homework. "Oh, Angela, no!" exclaimed Sara in dismay. "Not *all* of them!"

"Not every single one of them," conceded Angela grudgingly. "Not math, of course, and not French, cause it's so close to Spanish. With to hell they'd've let me take Spanish. But English is a definite wipe. History too, probably. I *hate* history!"

Sara winced. Apart from her beloved Latin, history was her greatest passion. "But, Angela, how can you hate history? It's everything there is to know!"

"It's just a bunch of dead people and dead dates," growled Angela. She was in a foul mood because only this morning, in the cold light of day, she had realized how little she'd absorbed from her classes in the last few weeks. The trouble she was in now was of her own making; she had nobody to blame but herself.

Caught up in an ongoing passionate relationship with Mickey, lulled into confidence by Tucker, Angela had been neglecting her schoolwork, relying on being able to squeak by with Missy Farina's homework and Stacey Underhill's term papers. But exams were different. There she had nothing to rely upon except herself and what she'd learned, and she'd already done miserably on two pop quizzes.

Now midterms were only a week away, and Angela realized too late that she was doomed.

"Even mathematics is a part of history," continued Sara. "Every great mathematical discovery, from the first numbers in the Egypt of thirty-five hundred B.C., to the calculations of the Babylonian astronomers, to the invention of zero, to Arabic numerals, to the theory of relativity are part of history," lectured Sara, now in her element. "Euclidean geometry is history; non-Euclidean gemoetry is history."

"What the hell are you talking about?" Angela scowled impatiently. "What do you mean, 'the invention of zero'?"

"It was a long time before mathematicians recognized the importance of the concept of the zero or negative numbers. An Indian mathematician was the first, but that wasn't until the year one thousand A.D. But decimal points were used as long ago as ancient Crete, in the palace at Knossos. When the nation of Islam arose from the Dark Ages of Europe and studied ancient Greek science and mathematics, the Arabs carried it to Europe in the tenth century, along with the Indian system of numbers we now call Arabic numerals. Without the Greeks, you'd still be counting on your fingers, and without the Arabs, you'd still be counting Roman style, using two X's for twenty. The Arabs invented algebra too."

Angela stood flabbergasted, her mouth open, as little Sara poured out this flood of information nonstop. "How the hell do you know all this stuff?" she demanded.

Sara allowed herself a little smile. "It's all there is to know," she said simply. "History covers everything, even music and poetry and rock video and Cabbage Patch dolls."

Angela uttered a low whistle. "Boy, I wish you could get all that junk into my head in time for the midterm."

The little smile widened and became a grin. "If you'll stop calling it junk, I'll be happy to try. What are you studying for your midterm, European history?"

"Yeah." Angela sighed, nodding glumly. "All three thousand years of it."

"Would you like to begin right now?"

"Why not?" Angela shrugged. "I've already wasted enough time as it is."

Sara Grundfest pushed her glasses up on her little beaky nose. "Get your notebook," she ordered happily. "We'll start with the rise of the city-state. The first thing you have to understand is that cities don't just grow up out of nowhere. They arise only when the population of a country has grown enough food to feed itself *plus* others who aren't farmers. Then men and women are freed from agriculture, and they have time to learn, and build, and practice politics, and keep a standing army, so cities come into being."

Suddenly fascinated, Angela nodded and began to scribble furiously in her notebook.

" . . . and so the French were so darn mad at the Prussians for defeating them in the Franco-Prussian War of 1870 that they stripped Germany of everything after the armistice in 1918, and the resulting incredible poverty and unemployment and inflation in Germany allowed Hitler to rise to power, which led inevitably to World War Two," finished Sara at last.

"Wow!" breathed Angela, putting down her pencil, exhausted. The two of them had worked four hours a day for the last three days, covering all the territory in Angela's textbook. Angela and Sara had done nothing but eat and drink history, immersing themselves in people and ideas, the rise of nations and their fall, the role played by religions and science, the development of technology and the Industrial Revolution, the shifting balances of power, dreadful and crippling wars, revolutions and bloodshed.

"Wow!" said Angela again. "It all fits together, doesn't it?"

Sara laughed, a happy though tired laugh. "That's what I wanted you to see. Not dead dates and dead people, but living events caused by living people, following each other day by day, following the laws of cause and effect up until 1986. People make history, not the other way around.

That's what the Romans called history—*res gestae*, the doings of people."

Angela stood up and stretched her long body, kneading her tired shoulder and neck muscles to get the kinks out of them. For three long days she'd been cooped up in this little room with Sara Grundfest, not seeing Tucker, not even taking Mickey's calls. Nothing but history was important. Now, the patterns as they repeated themselves down the ages were as clear to her as a simple equation. She'd learned it, thanks to Sara.

"Thanks, roomie, thanks a lot. I think we made some history here too."

Sara glowed with satisfaction. Like the mouse in the fable, she'd been able to help the lion. It was what she'd wanted wholeheartedly since the first day that Angela had come marching into their room and thrown her suitcase on the bed.

"Yes, I think you've got a pretty good grasp of the subject now," she answered. "You might miss some of the short-answer questions, dates and all that, but I think you'll do extremely well on the essays. But what about the English midterm?"

"Oh, no!" wailed Angela. "I can't face it, I swear I can't. Take it away."

"Angela," stated Sara so firmly she surprised herself, "your grade point and your scholarship are at stake here. Go and take a five-minute break. Just sneak a cigarette, then come right back in here and say hello to Mr. Textbook!"

"I cannot b*elieve* you, Angela. You refuse my help, you lock yourself in your room with that ink-stained little . . . *thing.*"

"Watch what you say about Sara," retorted Angela through grim lips. "She's been a good friend to me, Tucker. A very good friend. Plus she knows everything there is to know about history and English."

"And what am *I*? Guacamole dip?" demanded an indignant Tucker Tuckerman.

"No, you're temptation, and I can't afford that, with only two more days to go before midterms. You know damn well that every time we get together to study, we wind up counting your cashmeres or fixing each other's hair or gassing about boys—sorry—*men*. I have a great time with you, Tuck, but it's not helping me get through my exams. If I screw up, it's back to the Bronx for Angela Torres, *adíos*, and *hasta luego*."

Angela pushed back her dining-room chair and stood up, ignoring the rest of the food on her tray. "Everything comes easy for you, Tucker, because you grew up in a house with books, where everybody went to college. Me, I didn't even talk English until I was five years old and started school. All this stuff is new to me, and I'm even getting to like it. Sara is an awesome teacher, she has a real gift. After midterms, I'll be back, I promise. Only I won't be able to take as much goof-off time as I did before. I really care about Holly Hills now, and I want to stay here."

Anthea Tuckerman sniffed and her cat eyes narrowed to slits. "Maybe I won't be in such a hurry to take you back," she retorted angrily.

Angela looked at her for a long moment, then shrugged. "Suit yourself," she said quietly, hurt. "You will, anyway. You always do suit yourself. I know I couldn't throw a friend away that easily, like a used-up Kleenex." With that, she left to go back to Sara and Mr. Textbook.

"What the hell is going on, Angela? Suddenly, it's the Big Chill. You won't see me, you won't even take my calls. Are you going out with somebody else?" Mickey's voice crackled with anger over the phone.

Angela was too tired and nervous over the next day's exams to watch what she was saying; her first reaction was anger because Mickey was mistrusting her. Didn't he know that she missed him as much as he missed her?

"Hey, back off! Give me some room, Paco. I'm talking to you now, aren't I?"

"Big furry deal," grumbled Mickey. "You'd think we

didn't mean anything to each other . . . *you* know, hon. I just miss my girl, that's all."

"Mickey, it's midterms, man. They're tomorrow, and I'm hurtin' bad. I've never been so scared of anything in my life before, or . . . almost," said Angela, remembering the one horrendous time in her life that was even more terrifying than the ordeal of the exams. "Just wish me luck, baby, right?"

"Well, but when can I see you?" Mickey lowered his voice so that he wouldn't be overheard. "I'm hot for you, Angela. So hot it's burning me up. I think about you all the time, the way you look, the way we—"

"Mickey, don't put that in my face now, okay? Don't make it harder for me than it already is. I got other things on my mind. More important things." The minute the words left her lips, Angela knew they were a mistake, and she wished she could recall them. What she meant to say was that she missed Mickey as much as he missed her, maybe even more, but that she simply couldn't allow herself to think about him until exams were over and she was home free.

But that wasn't the way it came out. What she'd said was like a slap in his face, and now it was too late to change her words. Mickey Harrison was really angry.

"Squash that, Angela. This whole *relationship,*" and he underscored the word with heavy sarcasm, "is a wipeout. Let's just forget it." The phone clicked sharply in her ear.

Angela hung the phone up slowly. She didn't understand; she simply didn't understand people like Tucker and Mickey. They always wanted everything their own way and right away. They wouldn't yield an inch, not an inch, to the needs of others. They were selfish and spoiled, Angela realized. So why were they so damn attractive?

When Angela opened her history exam booklet and looked at the questions, she drew a total blank. Even the words themselves didn't make sense to her. It was as though they were in a foreign language that she'd never learned. No hope.

She would have given anything for a cigarette at that moment; her lungs ached for the harsh invasion of the smoke, and her hands trembled on her pen. Closing her eyes, Angela drew a deep breath and counted slowly to ten. Then, suddenly, she heard Sara's clear voice in her head. "If it weren't for the Arabs, you'd be counting in Roman numbers."

Angela looked back down at the paper, and every word that Sara Grundfest had hammered into her head came rushing back to her now. She picked up her pen and began to write, and write, and write. . . .

Two hours later, Angela was astonished to hear the bell ring, signaling the end of the history midterm. The minutes had simply flown by! She had filled one exam booklet and most of a second, and she handed both of them in with flushed cheeks and a pounding heart.

I think I did well, but who knows? she thought. Yet now she felt hope where before there had been none. This afternoon she'd be taking the English exam, and she believed that what Sara had taught her would stick. She felt almost confident as she walked slowly to Laurel Dorm, not seeing any of the girls who waved a greeting to her. Her thoughts were elsewhere, lost in a sense of shame. Shame that she had treated her own roommate so badly for all these weeks, ignoring her, not defending her when the girls in Tucker's clique made nasty little disparaging remarks about her, calling Sara "dork," "geek," "juice box," and other absurd, mean-spirited names. Shame that she had neglected that most precious thing, her own education, her ticket out. Look where her neglect had almost got her!

Man, she owed Sara Grundfest one. One! She owed her at least two! Angela was determined to find a way to pay Sara back for everything she'd done for her. As soon as midterms were over. There had to be a way.

"I heard you had a fight with Mickey Harrison. I couldn't be happier about it," drawled the lazy voice on the phone.

"Who's this?" demanded Angela.

The voice sighed dramatically. "How quickly they forget! And I was so sure I'd made An Impression."

Now something in the voice was so familiar to her that Angela began to laugh. "Pepper, right? Tucker's brother?"

Another deep sigh. "The cross I bear through life, being identified as 'Tucker's brother' by beautiful women on seven continents."

"Don't let it make you crazy, man. There's gotta be some part of the civilized world where Tucker is known as Pepper Tuckerman's sister."

"If there is, let us fly there together, my Angel. You got the wings for it, I'll tell the world."

"You talk a lot for a dude who hasn't said anything yet," remarked Angela.

"How's about a date Saturday night? Is that concise enough for you? If you're not dating Mickey Harrison, and the grapevine says it's off between you, then how about dating me? I'm not contagious, except for my wit and charm."

"What else does the grapevine say?" asked Angela nervously. Had Mickey been shooting his mouth off about her all over Cumberland Prep? Was that why Tucker's brother was on the phone right now? Because he'd heard that Angela Torres was easy?

"It says that Harrison is heartbroken, and is soon to forswear women entirely and enter a monastery. Can't say that I blame him, or that I'll lift a finger to stop him. What do you say, beautiful Angela? Would you like to go dancing on Saturday night? I'll take you to a juice disco where everybody goes, and we can break a few records. Let your light shine on me. Please?"

He *was* charming, no two ways about it. Pepper's big rep as a ladies' man had been earned in battle, and he knew all the moves. The minute he'd heard about the breakup between Mickey and Angela Torres, wheels had begun to turn in his hot little brain. If the Lord had made more than one Angela Torres, Pepper Tuckerman hadn't met her yet. So he wanted the only one he'd ever seen.

"Let me think a minute," answered Angela cagily. She was tempted, very tempted, but there was something about Pepper she didn't quite trust. He was as slick as glass, you could iceskate on his skin. Probably the most fun a girl could have on a date, but not somebody you'd entrust life and limb to, let alone heart and soul.

Yet she was curious about him, about his reputation, and not only because he was Tucker's brother but because he was dynamite looking. Her heart was still torn between Sam and Mickey, but one of them was far away and the other wasn't talking to her. Maybe if she made Mickey Harrison a little jealous . . .

Suddenly, an idea flashed into her mind. A brilliant idea, a phenomenal idea. "Say, do you know Lindsay Hagen?" she asked him. "He goes to Cumberland, doesn't he?"

"Hagen? Sure, he's in my class. But he's no match for you, precious. He's what we call an academic. Totally wrapped up in his studies. Why do you ask?"

"I was thinking that, if he's free, you could bring him along, and we could double-date with my roommate."

"Double-date? You can't be serious! That's like dragging around a hundred pounds of flopping flounder! I thought we could get off by ourselves somewhere."

"Double or nothing. Take it or leave it," stated Angela with the utmost cool.

"I'll take it," Pepper put in hastily. "What's your roommate like? I don't even know who she is."

"Her name is Sara Grundfest."

"Why do I hear a somber bell tolling in the distance?" complained Pepper. "I thought I knew every girl at Holly Hills, but this Sara What's-her-face is a new one on me. She's gotta be deadly, right?"

"Wrong!" Angela took a deep breath. It wasn't *exactly* a lie. "She's very nice." At least that part was true.

Pepper surrendered. "It's no gristle off my whistle," he said at last. "But what if Hagen doesn't go for it?"

"Then I don't go for it. Double or nothing, *chico*. Double or nothing."

"He'll be there," agreed Pepper grimly. "If I have to drug him and drag him, he'll be there."

"Solid!" Angela hung up the phone, pleased with herself. Now all I have to do is convince Sara, she thought, and that ain't gonna be so easy.

CHAPTER NINE

A True Friend

"Not easy" turned out to be an understatement. Informing Sara of the plans she'd made for the two of them was more of an ordeal than Angela had anticipated.

"No! Absolutely not!" Sara had shrieked when she heard what Angela was proposing. "No, it's impossible! I can't!"

"Hey, c'mon, why not? I'm not asking you to walk blindfolded off the top of the World Trade Center. It's only one date, for God's sake, one crappy little date."

The smaller girl kept shaking her head back and forth so vehemently that the ends of her braids whipped into her glasses. "I won't do it!" she yelled. "You can't make me!" she yelled. "If it's so crappy, why do you want to go?" she yelled. She seemed quite genuinely terrified at the prospect.

"Hey, chill out!" Angela raised her hands, palms up, helplessly. "Nobody's trying to *make* you do anything, damn it! All I wanted was maybe to show you a good time, pay you back a little for getting my ass through the midterms in one piece. This just seemed like a good opportunity, that's all. It's no big deal. But if you don't want to . . ."

"I don't want to," said Sara more quietly, but with equal firmness, and Angela was astonished to see tears forming behind the lenses of her roommate's thick glasses.

"Okay, then," said Angela curtly, slapping her headphones on and slamming a tape into her Walkman. The gesture was total dismissal of Sara, and it didn't go unnoticed. It hurt.

She doesn't understand at all, said Sara Grundfest to herself mournfully. How could she? She's never been homely and she's never been shy. She doesn't know how painful it is to be like me. To be afraid of new people. To freeze and stammer and want to run away and hide. Doesn't she even stop to consider how bizarre the two of us would look standing next to each other? She's so tall and beautiful, and me, I'm just . . . a field mouse in glasses. Why, any boy in his right mind would take only one look and disappear in a puff of indignant smoke. How could I stand to be rejected like that in front of anybody, especially Angela? It would destroy me.

I didn't mean to freak her out so bad, thought Angela. Who knew she was that paranoid? That shyness of hers is a real crippler; how the hell does she expect to get through life in that head? No matter how many master's degrees or doctorates she piles up, sooner or later, she's going to have to leave school and go out in the world, and then, look out, Sara Grundfest! It's gonna be get-real time, and she won't be ready for it. I feel sorry for her.

But there seemed nothing for Angela to do, and no way she could help. She and Sara had effectively cut each other off, so Angela turned up the volume and allowed the music to wash over her.

With a sigh, Sara Grundfest burrowed among her possessions until she found her own tape player. She inserted a prized and beloved cassette and adjusted the headphones.

For four or five minutes the two of them sat in silence, each girl locked away with her music unheard by the other, a living portrait of isolation and loneliness. Then Sara broke the silence.

"Angela?"

But Angela didn't hear her, because the music in her ears was so loud.

"Angela?" And this time, Sara touched her gently on the arm and mouthed for her to take off the muffs.

"Yo, what's happening?"

"Um, I was thinking . . . do you like classical music?"

"Say what?"

"You know, Bach, Mozart."

Angela shrugged. "Dunno. Never heard any, at least I don't think I did."

Sara smiled shyly. "Oh, you'd know if you heard it. It's just that . . . I'm listening now to something so beautiful, and I'd love to share it with you." She looked hopefully at her roommate.

Inside, Angela winced. The last thing she wanted to hear was old, dead, boring music. But she recognized the gesture for what it was, Sara reaching out, and Angela knew she ought to accept. It was the least she could do.

"Why not? Let's have it, whatever it is."

Eagerly, little Sara rewound the tape to the beginning. "It's Bach's Sonata in G Minor," she informed Angela.

Estupendo, thought Angela sourly. Terrific. She took the cassette from Sara, slipped it into her own player, slipped her muffs back on, and hit the play button.

Immediately, the world of pure mathematics was turned into crystalline sound. The most beautiful music that Angela Torres had ever heard in all her sixteen years came pouring like molten silver into her ears. The complexity of the minor chords reminded her of the most tantalizing equations, and they rippled through Angela's willing head as they built a vaulted, turreted castle of melody and harmony that seemed to encompass everything wonderful.

"Estupendo," breathed Angela, but this time it wasn't sarcasm. Her face, lit up by joy, turned to smile happily at Sara, thanking her for this surprising and astonishing gift.

Sara smiled back, suffused with her own joy that Angela heard and Angela understood. Not a word was spoken until the tape came to an end and Angela, reluctantly, took off the headphones.

"Whew! That was outstanding." She sighed. "What did you say the name of it was?"

"Sonata in G Minor, by Johann Sebastian Bach."

"This guy Bach, he write other things?"

"Oh, yes, he was *very* prolific. I have a lot of tapes you can listen to. And Mozart too. Symphonies, quartets, concertos . . . If you love Bach, you'll love Mozart. And Vivaldi, and Corelli, and Haydn and Boccherini—"

"Hey, hold it!" Laughing, Angela put up one hand. "Give me a break! Don't throw everything at me all at once. One thing at a time. When do I get to eat or sleep?"

"I'm so happy you liked the music. I thought you would, because it's . . . it's like you, somehow."

"Yeah? How do you figure that?" asked Angela curiously.

"Well, for one thing, it's precise . . . that's the mathematical part of you. But it's strong and beautiful and honest—" Sara broke off, blushing, afraid she'd said too much.

Angela blushed too, but for a different reason entirely. Her own selfishness put her to same. She had dared to be angry when Sara refused to go out, angry because Angela really did want to date Pepper Tuckerman, and she had already gone and painted herself into a corner—no double date, no Pepper. She'd been using Sara without giving any thought to the feelings of the other girl. I don't deserve any of the good words that Sara is dishing out to me, she thought. I haven't acted strong or honest; I haven't acted like a friend.

She wished there was something she could do for Sara, some gift equal to the beautiful music Sara had just given her. A sudden thought struck her. "Hey, Sara, do you dig rock'n'roll?"

"What?" The large eyes behind the glasses widened, and Sara gave a little shiver of distaste. "No, I hate it! It's just barbaric loud noise!"

"Yeah, well, I have to admit a lot of it is pretty loud. But a lot of it is real music too. Like the Beatles, for instance. I have tapes of some early stuff, folk rockers like Simon and Garfunkel, Judy Collins. I think you'd enjoy them if only you'd kick back and give them a listen."

But Sara kept shaking her head. "No, I wouldn't. I'm certain I wouldn't."

"Hey, I listened to *your* music, didn't I? *And* I loved it. Now it's your turn. Give it a chance, okay? You can always press the stop button and shut it right off. That's what life is all about, having options. C'mon, whaddya say? Please . . ."

It was impossible for Sara to resist further. Not after Angela Torres had actually said please. So she gritted her teeth and nodded.

"I'll go easy on you." Angela smiled. "I promise not to blast the top of your head off with U-2 or Van Halen. Just try this." Finding the tape she wanted, she inserted it, switched it on, turned the volume down and put the earphones over Sara's head.

The girl listened for a minute or two, then a small smile of enjoyment tugged at the corners of her lips. Pressing the pause button, she took off the muffs. "Why, it's pretty! Really melodious! The harmonics are excellent, it's well orchestrated, and even the lyrics are poetic. What do you call it?"

"A golden oldie, kid. It's the Beatles, *Revolver.*"

"I like it, I actually like it. 'Eleanor Rigby' was just beautiful. I'm going to listen to the rest of it, if you don't mind."

"Be my guest. As a matter of fact, why don't you take off those phones? I'd like to listen too."

For half an hour the two of them sat silent as the melodies wove a pattern of bright happy sweetness around the room, wrapping them in a bond of sisterly serenity. Angela had to laugh when Sara actually tapped her feet to the music.

When the album was finished, Sara Grundfest sighed deeply.

"Angela, about that date you wanted to fix me up with . . . I'd like to explain how I feel . . ."

"Hey, *de nada.* You don't owe me any explanation. I was out of line, that's all."

"No, that's not all. It's just that . . . well, I've seen some of the boys that come here to Holly Hills to date the girls. All they're interested in is a pretty face and a good body. Or else they go for the airheads. That leaves me out. I don't fit into either category, none of those boys would ever be interested in me. So why should I stand still for getting rejected and hurt? I know I'm not pretty. I'm used to that . . . sort of. But why should I have my nose rubbed in it? I'm better off as I am now. I'm not always lonely . . . only sometimes."

Angela nodded. "I'm sorry. I wasn't thinking. But I don't think all boys are like that. I think some of them must be deeper than you say, and have a better sense of values. I mean, they're people too, right? For example, this Linday Hagen I wanted you to meet. I met him once and he's not really like the others. He's more serious and a lot smarter. Also, I think he's on the sensitive side, like you are."

But Sara still shook her head. "What could he possibly see in me?"

"Hey, don't sell yourself short. You make Sara Grundfest sound like something scraped off the bottom of a running shoe. You're not that bad, *chica*. You're even . . . kind of good-looking."

"Hah!" cried Sara bitterly. She knew better.

"No, listen. You got some nice features. But do you always have to wear your hair that way? In two pigtails, like Pocahontas?"

One ink-stained finger reached up to touch the braids tentatively. "I always have. Ever since I was five years old."

"So what does that mean, that you have to keep on doing it? Take off those rubber bands, and let's see what we have here." Angela reached for Sara's hair.

"Ow! You're pulling! Let me do it. There!"

Sara's hair, freed of the braids, fluffed out around her head, all wavy from being plaited, the color of soft brown. It was very beautiful, very pre-Raphaelite, like the hair of a young girl in a Burne-Jones painting.

"See, dummy? You got gorgeous hair, and you've been hiding it for years! Take a look at yourself in the mirror. Uh, can you see without those glasses?"

"Not even an elephant if he were waltzing under my nose."

"Okay, leave 'em on. What the hell, Lindsay Hagen wears glasses too."

"Now, Angela, I never told you I would go."

"Yeah, sure, I know. What about clothes. You got anything jazzy, like tight jeans?"

"Jeans? No. I don't own a pair. I've never worn anything but very plain dresses and skirts. I wouldn't be comfortable in anything else."

"Got any money?"

"Um, yes. About forty dollars. I hardly spend my allowance on anything but books."

"Well, you're about to spend forty bucks on something else for a change. Something pretty to wear. And I don't trust you, so I'm coming along. You got a cute little body, you know that? Skinny, but foxy. You should dress to show it off."

"Angela!" A look of real shock crossed Sara's face.

"Hey, with that hair and your cute little bod, you can even get away with the glasses. Matter of fact, they sort of suit you, although we're gonna have to go shopping for some sexier frames. Smear a little blusher and mascara and lipstick on you, and you won't break any mirrors."

But Sara was shaking her head stubbornly. "Forget it, Angela, I'm not going! And that's final!"

Angela played her ace.

"Hey, I just remembered something. You know that Latin you always got your nose stuck in? That old dead language that nobody human needs? Well, this Lindsay Hagen is as big a loony tune as you. He's studying the same boring stuff you are. Told me something about digging in the ground, finding old dinosaur bones. Tell the truth, I didn't listen very hard."

That last statement was something of a fib; Angela had liked and respected Lin on their only meeting and remembered everything he had said to her. But she decided that Sara would rise up in Latin's defense, and that some of her defense would spill over onto Lindsay Hagen. She was right.

"You're so wrong, Angela! Latin is far from dead and boring! It's alive and thrilling! You should have listened to every word he said; maybe you would have learned something new! And you shouldn't put Latin down, Angela. If it hadn't been for Latin, there would *be* no Spanish language!"

Angela laughed. "That's where you're wrong. There would always *have* to be Spanish. It's the language of love, *chica,* the language of *amor.* But I get your point." She shrugged and turned away, pretending that the conversation was over, but she kept one eye peeled on Sara.

Sara kept sneaking peeks at herself in the mirror, hoping Angela wouldn't notice. Once she put her hands up to her loosened fluff of hair and smoothed it a little. That's when Angela Torres knew she had won. It was all over but the shopping.

It was a different kind of victory from what she'd expected when she'd demanded earlier that Sara make up the foursome. Then she'd been thinking only of herself, of her desire to know the legendary Pepper Tuckerman better and make Mickey Harrison jealous.

But in the last hour of this afternoon, something had happened between Angela Torres and Sara Grundfest. They had become friends. Sara was like the *pequeños,* the younger kids who always flocked around Angela for advice and protection. She was a *pequeña,* and it was up to Angela to watch over her like an older sister. Now, she wanted to bring her out of her shell, to help Sara function in the real world. As she always used to do, Angela Torres accepted the responsibility of a new friendship.

Besides, it suddenly occurred to her for the first time that maybe, just maybe, Sara Grundfest and Lindsay Hagen might hit it off, after all.

CHAPTER TEN

Miracles

By Saturday night, they had accomplished miracles. A pretty mohair sweater and matching skirt had been paid for and wrapped up, over Sara's squeaky protests that they were too tight and that she would never wear them. A little bag of very simple pale-colored cosmetics was toted up from the village by a triumphant Angela.

"Stop squirming, damn it!" snapped Angela. "Do you want me to smear this blusher onto your nose?"

"I can't help it," moaned Sara. "It feels funny. I never wore anything on my face before."

"It's too bad you haven't got contacts. Your eyes are really very pretty, especially with a little makeup. I never saw eyes that color before, gray and brown mixed. And you have good cheekbones. You know, I like doing this. My sisters always used to let me fuss with their hair and makeup before they moved out and got married. I suppose that if I ever flunk out of Holly Hills and have to kiss astrophysics *adiós,* I can always make a living in a beauty salon."

"Don't say that!" cried a horrified Sara. "Don't ever say a thing like that! You mustn't *ever* give up your education. You have a *brilliant* mind, and you mustn't even dream of letting it go to waste."

But Angela merely pulled the towel from off her roommate's neck and said, in her best classroom French, "*Voilà!*"

Sara nervously peered into the mirror. All she could see

without her glasses was a blur. Putting them on, she took a long look at herself while her heart beat faster.

"My goodness," she whispered. "My goodness."

In one of Sara's favorite novels, *Northanger Abbey,* the heroine overhears her parents remarking that "She is almost pretty today." Jane Austen goes on to write, "To look *almost* pretty is an acquisition of higher delight to a girl who has been looking plain the first fifteen years of her life than a beauty from her cradle can ever receive."

Those words came back in full force to Sara as she studied her reflection. With joy, she realized that she was almost pretty. The little bookworm had been transformed, if not into a butterfly, then at least into a lovely moth with feathery wings.

Even behind the thick glasses, her eyes looked wider, the lashes thickened and lengthened by a touch of mascara. The lip gloss heightened the contours of her mouth and the blusher brought color to her white cheeks, pale from having lived an indoor life for so long. The fluffy sweater fitted smoothly, its dusty rose color now softening Sara's small chest and thin shoulders.

But it was her hair that was a triumph, both for Sara and for Angela. There was so much of it that Angela had been able to be creative, pulling some of it away from Sara's face and holding it with bright plastic clips, fluffing out the rest and letting it fall wherever it would. It was magnificent; it had never been cut and it rippled in gentle waves halfway down to Sara's tiny waist.

"Well?" demanded Angela, grinning.

"I . . . I don't know what to say. Is that me?"

"That's you, kid. And it always was. Keep thinking that it's you and you can wash all that stuff off your face and it will *still* be you."

"Yo, Angela." Stacey Underhill was standing suddenly in the doorway of their room, staring in disbelief at Sara Grundfest.

"What's happening?"

"Tucker wants to see you."

Angela bristled. "No shit? Then how come she sent you? How come she didn't toddle on over here herself and just say hi? She knows where to find me."

But she already knew the answer to that one. The princess lifts a finger and the slaves move it on the double. Tucker says "squat" and the Three Stooges start straining. I thought we were friends, Angela said to herself. I thought she was above that kind of shit with me. I guess I was wrong. I guess she must think I'm one of her stooges.

Suddenly, Angela was tired of that whole scene. Tired of the ass-licking and the clones and bored with Anthea Tuckerman's superior attitude.

"Well, you can just race on back to *Ms*. Tuckerman and tell her I'm busy, and I'm going out. No, tell her *we're* going out." And she draped one protective arm around Sara's shoulders, feeling pretty damn good about reclaiming some of the old Angela Torres independence.

"And *then* she said that you could go to hell for all she cared, but she was going out, and it wasn't going to be with you but with that squid of a roommate of hers, who by the way, wasn't looking as totally gross as she usually does," finished Jennifer, out of breath, having distorted the truth as maliciously as she could.

Tucker's cat eyes had snapped open in disbelief at Jennifer Ripley's narrative; now they closed again to narrow slits through which only a glimmer of icy green showed. "In*deed!*" was all she whispered, but it was enough to send a shiver down Missy Farina's little frightened back.

"I thought she broke up with Mickey Harrison," Stacey Underhill put in.

"Who do you suppose she's going out with?" wondered the nosy Jennifer Ripley out loud.

The Three Stooges were actually enjoying Tucker Tuckerman's discomfort, knowing that Angela hadn't been around for several days and had made plans which not only didn't include Tucker, the sophomore-class idol, but which did, incredibly, include Sara Grundfest, the sophomore-class turkey!

"Never mind wondering," snapped Anthea Tuckerman. "Find out! And this time get it right!"

Angela hadn't been out dancing in weeks, and her feet were just itching to get out and get down. With midterms over and the Thanksgiving break less than a week away, she was high and floating and free, just on energy alone. It didn't occur to her until she and Pepper hit the floor that neither Sara nor Lindsay knew how to dance. Left behind, the two of them just kept sitting there—in the middle of all those decibels that were pouring from the huge disco speakers—silent and looking miserable.

One pang of guilt, and then the other two were forgotten and Angela and Pepper began shaking their booty. He was a super dancer, light, graceful, agile as a cat. He made it look easy.

Sara had never been so miserable in her life. All her efforts and Angela's attempts to make her "almost pretty" seemed to go for nothing. It wouldn't have mattered to Lindsay Hagen if she'd painted herself blue and wore nothing but a loincloth and a necklace of bears' teeth. When they were introduced, he said a polite hello and looked through Sara as though she were a pane of window glass, staring all the while with longing eyes at Angela. He'd been staring at her ever since.

What hurt the most is this: if Sara Grundfest were ever to be attracted to a boy, which at this moment in time she sincerely doubted, Lindsay Hagen was exactly the kind of boy to attract her. He wasn't intimidatingly handsome; instead he had a good-natured, serious, sensitive face, a little owlish behind his glasses, just like Sara's own face. He was quiet and had gentle manners. He didn't know how to dance, and he was very obviously as allergic as she was to the decibel level of the synthetically amplified noise in the crowded teenage disco. In fact, Lindsay Hagen was perfect, except for one thing. He hadn't given Sara a second look, reserving all his attention for Angela.

He was watching her now as she spun gracefully around the crowded dance floor with Pepper Tuckerman. Sara sighed. Who could blame him for preferring Angela Torres to Sara Grundfest? It seemed to her the most natural thing in the world.

Were they just going to sit here all evening, unable to say a word to each other because of the noise? Sara's head was already beginning to ache, and she was feeling like a dressed-up fool in her mohair sweater and lip gloss. She had to do something or she'd go crazy. Most of all, she needed a long gulp of fresh air.

She stood up. "I'm going outside for a minute," she told Lin.

"Say what?" He cupped one hand to his ear, indicating that he couldn't hear her over the music.

"I have to go out for *air*!" she shouted, and moved off.

She never expected that he would actually follow her outside, but he did, no doubt only out of a sense of politeness.

It was a chilly but clear evening in mid-November. A waning moon, still three-quarters full, shone from high in the sky, pale and silver. The wind soughed in the branches of the pine trees that grew around the disco, which stood on a remote Connecticut road a few miles from Holly Hills.

"Oh, that's much better," declared Lindsay, taking a deep breath of the fresh air. "I was starting to get the headache that ate Dubuque."

"Me too," confessed Sara. "I'll never get used to music as loud as that. I can't even think of it as music. It's just noise!"

"Yeah," agreed Lin, but he cast a somewhat longing glance back at the disco, in the direction, Sara knew, of Angela Torres. For a long minute, the two stood silent, each of them too shy to say anything to the other. "Damn," said Sara under her breath, cursing her humiliating shyness; she really liked this boy, but she didn't stand a chance with him.

"Uh, I didn't get your last name when we were introduced," said Lindsay with some embarrassment.

"Grundfest, Sara Grundfest."

"Grundfest!" His owlish face lit up suddenly. "Are you related, by any chance, to Cornelia and Icarus Grundfest?"

"Less by chance than by capricious nature," replied Sara with a small smile. "They are my mother and father."

Behind his glasses, Lindsay Hagen's eyes were round in astonishment. "But I thought they were . . . um . . . older."

"You don't have to be embarrassed," Sara replied softly. "They *are* older than most parents with a daughter my age. My father was fifty and my mother was forty-five when I was born." The thought always saddened her that in the natural course of things she would probably lose them relatively early in her life.

"I can't believe it! They're your parents! That's so far out! I mean, your father's translation of *The Odyssey* is like my bible! It's brilliant! And his lectures on Catullus! And your mother's book about the tribal migrations of the Aryans . . . Wow! Far out! I really envy you. You're so lucky!"

His enthusiasm was infectious, and it made Sara grin broadly. "Yes, I'm lucky and I know it. Growing up in a house dedicated to scholarship, surrounded by books and music and people who cared more for ideas than for things . . . well, it was nurturing and wonderful, and I'm very grateful."

For the first time, Lindsay Hagen took a good look at Sara Grundfest. And he liked what he saw. A sweet face, not intimidatingly pretty, but with good bones and large, shining, intelligent eyes. A small, neat body, like a little kitten's, in that fuzzy sweater she was wearing.

"You're studying Latin, of course," he said to her.

"Of course. *And* Greek."

"Me too." Lin's smile grew broader. "This semester it's Plato. Have you read Plato?"

Sara's nose wrinkled a little scornfully. "Yes. The *Phaedo* and the *Crito*. I think that's enough."

"You don't like *Plato*!" Lindsay Hagen gasped in disbelief.

"Oh, the language is all right, I suppose, all those flowing phrases and that perfect correct Greek. But Socrates was such an old bore, with those pompous questions of his. And those toadies who kept following him around and letting him set them up. 'Yes, Socrates. No, Socrates. Oh, Socrates, you're so very wise, there is nobody like you.' You want to know who I feel sorry for? His wife Xanthippe, that's who! She's stuck at home with all the responsibilities, cooking, cleaning, raising the children on no money at all, while her husband, who doesn't bring in a penny, is off to the Agora, to philosophize with that merry band of brownnosers. Leaving poor Xanthippe to carry the load and the reputation throughout all recorded history of being a shrew! It's not fair! I would have come after him with a broom myself!"

By the time she'd finished her harangue, Lindsay Hagen was laughing so hard he was nearly choking. "I never heard anybody say a negative thing about Socrates before," he gasped, wiping his eyes. "You're a stone gas, you know that? Just wonderful."

"Well," grumbled Sara, her tiny hands still balled up into fists. "There's a lot more that I *could* say about Socrates, but I'll give it a rest. I'm not sure you could handle it."

This sent both of them off into gales of laughter. When they'd stopped laughing, Lindsay said thoughtfully, "You know, I came here tonight with only one thing on my mind. Do you know what that was?"

Sara dropped her eyes and whispered, "Angela Torres."

"That's right, you're pretty sharp. Angela Torres. What a dynamite lady! I really wanted to get to know her better, so that maybe she'd go out with me."

Biting her lip, Sara turned away so that Lindsay wouldn't see the tears forming in her eyes. Suddenly, she felt a warm, strong hand on her shoulder.

"Sara, look at me," said Lin quietly. "No, don't pull away. Turn around and look at me. I have something important to say to you and I can't say it to the back of your neck."

Sara turned to find Lin's eyes fixed on her, his face serious.

"She's still a dynamite lady, but I've changed my mind. She's wrong for me; for one thing, we'd have nothing to talk about, nothing to laugh over. I bet *she* couldn't criticize Socrates."

"She couldn't even *pronounce* Socrates," agreed Sara, a little unfairly.

"What I'm trying to tell you is that I'd like to go out with *you*. You're pretty dynamite yourself, lady. I'd like to see more of you, get to know you better. We seem to have a lot in common, including ideas about Socrates and admiration of your mother and father. I think that's more important than just the physical, don't you?"

"Oh yes!" breathed Sara.

"Not that I have anything against the physical . . ." And Lindsay Hagen's lips were suddenly pressed softly against Sara Grundfest's, and his arms moved gently around her, hugging her, although not too tightly.

Sara closed her eyes, giving herself up to the brief kiss. She could not believe this moment was real, that a boy she really liked was kissing her, saying romantic things to her, liking her back. Just the *clink* that their eyeglasses made when they kissed took her breath away and made her shiver.

"You're cold," said Lindsay, breaking off the kiss. "We'd better go inside."

"No!" Sara's response was instinctive. "I mean . . . it's so noisy, so crowded . . . the cigarette smoke . . ."

"I'm afraid we're Siamese twins with Pepper and Angela," answered Lindsay ruefully. "We came in Pepper's car, so we have to wait until they're ready to go back. Unless . . . do you like to walk?"

"Walk? Yes, I love to. Why?"

"We could walk back to Holly Hills, and I could wait

until Pepper brings Angela home. I figure it's about four miles, but the moon is quite bright, and a long walk will give us a chance to get to know each other better. What do you say?''

Suddenly nervous, Sara blurted out, "I have to tell you something, Lindsay. I don't really look like this."

"What? What are you saying?"

"I'm wearing lipstick and blusher and mascara, and Angela did my hair for me, and I don't really look like this underneath."

One more time, Lindsay Hagen threw his head back and laughed as though his sides would explode. "You're a stitch, Sara, I swear you're the funniest girl I ever met. Of course you look like that! How much difference can a few cosmetics make? You've got the prettiest hair I ever saw! It's all in your head, you know. You look like you think you look, better or worse depends on you."

"That's what Angela says."

"Then she's even smarter than I gave her credit for. What do you say, Sara? Are you up to walking a few miles down a moonlit country road with me?"

Over coals of fire, said Sara to herself. Out loud, all she said was, "We'd better leave them a note at the table so they don't get worried."

"Good thinking."

"Hey, fantastic! That leaves just you and me, darlin'." Pepper smiled when he read the note.

"We can boogie the night away." Angela glowed, very pleased with herself at the way things were working out for Sara. She'd drag that girl into the twentieth century yet!

"Well, no. I had a rather different set of plans," purred Pepper, looking like the cat who'd lunched on the family canary.

"Such as?" With one eyebrow raised, Angela waited to see exactly how much Pepper Tuckerman thought he could get away with. He was kind of adorable, though, with that lopsided smile and those big green eyes. Even Angela, who preferred black hair and dark brown eyes, had to acknowledge that this guy Pepper Tuckerman was *estupendo*.

"Such as a camel train to Beluchistan, a *slow* camel train. You would travel in a curtained litter, my lovely, so that no dog of a camel driver could set eyes on your beauty. If he did, I'd have his tongue torn out and thrown to the hyenas! Or perhaps a tramp streamer, traveling around the horn of Africa, you and me wrapped in blankets on steamer chairs, sipping bouillon, being mysterious. How about a ride on the Orient Express? The Magical Mystery Tour? How's about getting out of here and going somewhere where we can be alone together?"

"Why, you silver-tongued devil, you give a girl a thrill just to hear those romantic words. Thanks but no thanks; if it's all the same to you, I'd rather dance."

"Damn it, Angela! Why won't you give me a break?"

"For true, Pepper?"

"For true."

"Because if I've ever seen anybody who'd grab for the whole hand if you gave him a finger, that person is you, Pepper Tuckerman."

"What you're saying is that you don't trust me."

"No lie." Angela smiled.

Pepper's hand snaked out so swiftly that Angela never saw it coming. The next thing she knew he had her tightly by the wrist and had yanked her over to him. There, in the middle of the disco, dancers all around them, he crushed her lips to his, forcing his tongue between her teeth, pressing his powerful body against hers.

The kiss caught Angela by surprise. She tried to twist away from Pepper, but he held her firmly, his strong fingers digging into her wrist. The kiss deepened, and she allowed him to force her lips open as she began to kiss him back.

By the time Pepper let go of Angela's wrist, she had changed her mind about decking him. Instead, she wrapped that arm tightly around him, pulling him even closer.

At last, they broke apart, Angela breathing hard.

"And what I'm saying, Angela Torres, is that you don't trust yourself," said Pepper with a triumphant grin. "And for damn good reason. You want me as much as I want you. Now come on. Let's get the hell out of here."

CHAPTER ELEVEN

Terrible Trouble

"It's five minutes to eleven! Where on earth could they be? Angela is going to get into terrible trouble," whispered Sara anxiously. "If she's not signed in by eleven, they'll ground her, or maybe even worse. She's on scholarship, you know, and she simply mustn't jeopardize that! I'm so worried!"

Lindsay's arm tightened around her shoulders. "She'll be all right," he assured her, but without much conviction. "Pepper will see that she gets back safely."

Lindsay and Sara, tired and a little footsore, had arrived at the front gate of Holly Hills ten minutes earlier only to find no sign of Pepper and Angela. They sat huddled on the frozen ground around the side of the dorm, teeth chattering. Lin had taken his jacket off and wrapped it tightly around Sara, but the biting November wind penetrated to the girl's narrow bones.

She was freezing, she was terribly anxious about Angela, the ground was hard and rocky, yet Sara Grundfest had never been so happy in her life. She was afraid to put a name to this new feeling she was experiencing, but she knew that any amount of discomfort was bearable if it meant that she could spend five more minutes with Lindsay Hagen.

Their four-mile walk, down a wooded country road in the high, silver light of a waning autumn moon, had been the most thrilling experience of her life, even more wonderful than listening to Mozart or reading Shakespeare.

They'd talked for two hours, and for the first time in her

life, Sara Grundfest found it easy to be herself and express herself, to talk about what she really cared about. Before this, she never would have believed that conversation with a boy her own age could be so intelligent or enjoyable. But then, what other boy was like Lindsay? He was unique. He was interested in the things that shaped her very existence —the love of scholarship, the beauty of books and music, the poetry of Pindar and Catullus, the secret yearning for the glories of the past.

Yet Lin was all boy. He played on the Cumberland soccer team, he swam on the varsity team and competed with other schools, he loved movies and pop music—he kept raving about somebody he called "the Boss," who was a total mystery to Sara—and he was up on the latest slang. At Cumberland Prep, Lindsay Hagen was considered an academic because his grade-point average was so high and he was so serious about everything he undertook. Nevertheless, there was mischief in his soul. You can't come from a big family like his—three brothers and two sisters—without having picked up a sense of humor as a survival tool.

Being an only child, Sara saw things differently; her sense of humor had always been verbal rather than visual; she was fond of puns and cryptic puzzles, anagrams and difficult exercises in logic. Lin was good at all those things too, but he was also class champion at Space Invaders.

"I'll teach you," he'd promised. "It's all hand-eye coordination. It just takes practice."

An inner excitement gripped her, hearing that simple statement. It meant that Lindsay was taking it for granted that they'd be seeing each other again. It was what Sara wanted more than anything she could think of.

"I've got to go in now," she told him reluctantly. "It's two minutes of eleven. But how are you going to get back? Aren't you supposed to be back in school by eleven-thirty?"

"No problem." Lindsay grinned, helping her to her feet. "I'll run. It's only five miles and I've got half an hour."

"Run!" squeaked Sara, horrified. "But you can't!"

"Why not? I'm in pretty good shape. Don't smoke, don't drink, don't fool around . . . except with you, I hope."

Sara felt her knees shaking, and she might have fallen if Lindsay hadn't been holding her arm so tightly. "The road is so dark," she quavered. "Cars . . ."

"Hey, I'll be careful, I promise! I have no death wish, I assure you. Especially now, since I've met you." He walked her up to the front door and pushed her gently inside. "Now scamper home before you get into trouble."

"But Angela . . ." protested Sara.

"No buts, Sara. Angela will be all right. Pepper knows what he's doing." He leaned forward to kiss her lightly—he was almost a foot taller than she—and then he was off down the road, running easily. Sara watched him as long as she could, and as soon as he was out of sight, she turned with a heavy heart and went in. It was eleven on the nose, but still no sign of Angela Torres.

I hope Lin is right, Sara sighed to herself as she climbed the stairs to her room. I hope that Pepper knows what he's doing.

Pepper knew what he was doing, all right. He was trying to drive Angela Torres crazy with his kisses and caresses, trying to push her over the edge into no retreat.

Angela Torres had never been kissed like that before, so slowly and sensuously, as though all the time in the world was at their command, as though each kiss was going to last forever. In combat sex, Pepper Tuckerman had no equal.

Somehow they had wound up in the backseat of Pepper's BMW, parked in a lonely country lane many miles from Holly Hills. Thank heaven the seat wasn't any larger or more comfortable, or Angela might have been a goner. As it was, she'd already gone further than she'd intended. Even though it was feeling so good, it was time to call a halt.

For two hours, they'd been lying here together, kissing

and stroking each other with fingers of fire. The car was very warm, very dark and cosy, with a thin shaft of moonlight coming in through the window to outline their beautiful young bodies. Angela was more excited than she'd ever been—even with Sam—but something kept holding her back.

It was all too damn thrilling, too damn perfect. Weren't boys supposed to be more awkward and hasty, more fumbling and sincere? Pepper's lovemaking was a polished performance, as though it were a role he'd played many, many times.

I may be sorry about this some day, thought Angela as she pushed him away finally. *Pepper Tuckerman just might be the greatest lover in the universe. But not for me.*

"What's your problem, pretty lady?" he asked her as he felt her tighten her hands against his chest in her determination to push him away.

"What time is it?" she asked nervously.

"Why does it matter?" he drawled lazily. "C'mon back here. Pepper's getting lonely."

In a panic, Angela sat up. "Why does it matter? Are you loco? Show me your watch!" she demanded. "*Ay, Dios mío!* It's after eleven! I should have been back at school twenty minutes ago, and we're more than an hour away. Start the car, Pepper."

"Hey, what's your hurry? We're just getting off the ground here. This is only the warm-up, we haven't even made it to the field." He reached for her again.

"That's what *you* think, cowboy! I don't even know you." Angela was a strong girl, and when she pushed him out of the car, Pepper went flying. "Recess is over! Get your ass behind that wheel and drive like hell!" she yelled at him. "Or so help me God I'll total this thirty-five-thousand-dollar Krautmobile and you along with it."

Pepper Tuckerman may have been many things, but he wasn't a fool, and he knew the voice of authority when it barked in his ear. Switching on the engine without another word, he put the car into gear, and they were off.

Were all Latin girls at hot-tempered as Angela Torres?

Play with fire and you wind up with third-degree burns. Not for Carolina Tuckerman's little boy Piers-Paul. Congratulating himself on a narrow escape, Pepper started the car. It had certainly been an educational evening.

"All right!" yelled Anthea Tuckerman. "Where the hell is she?" Slamming the room door behind her, she stood for one moment in darkness, then snapped on the lights and ripped the blanket off Sara, who sat up blinking in astonishment mingled with fright.

Sara had never seen Tucker Tuckerman so angry. Actually, nobody had. Tucker never showed any emotion stronger than disdain. But now that she had let go, she was out of control and quite a terrifying sight. Her eyes shot twin bolts of green lightning; her cheeks, normally pale, were dark red with fury, and a vein pulsed in her forehead. She looked as though she was about to explode, like a boiler with no vent.

"Angela?" squeaked Sara.

"Of course Angela, you dimwit! Who the hell do you think I was talking about, Marie Antoinette?" Even furious, Tucker had class.

"I . . . she's late," stammered Sara.

"Tell me about it," snapped Tucker sarcastically. "Not only is she late, but she's out with my brother! With Pepper! Who or what gave her the right to go out with *my* brother? And wearing my best cashmere sweater too! Just wait until I get my hands on that Hispanic bitch! I'm going to throttle her."

Unused to being shouted at, Sara became a little confused. She wasn't sure what Tucker was angrier about, the brother or the sweater. "Why shouldn't she go out with Pepper? He asked her," she replied loyally.

Instantly, Anthea Tuckerman turned to ice. "I don't think you understand. My brother is a Tuckerman. That means something in this world. And he's not about to throw that something away on a . . . a . . . Puerto Rican!" The last words were filled with such contempt that Sara trembled and pulled the blanket back up to her ears.

Now Tucker had lost control of herself again, and her lips twisted cruelly. "Do you know the first English words a Puerto Rican baby learns?" She sneered. " 'Attention, K Mart shoppers.' " It was the meanest-spirited joke that Sara had ever heard, and it fired her indignation.

"Don't you dare talk about Angela Torres like that!" she yelled as loudly as she could. "Angela is brilliant and beautiful and wonderful. Why . . . why, even *you* made a friend of her!"

"A friend?" Tucker's golden eyebrow shot up. "Surely you're not serious. A girl like Angela Torres could never be my *friend*. A plaything, rather. She amused me, that's all. But I don't think it's amusing when a nobody from the slums makes a move on my brother. No, that's hardly a laughing matter, and Señorita Nobody is about to learn that lesson. When I get through with her, she's going to be sorry she ever laid eyes on either of the Tuckerman twins."

Whirling around, Tucker marched out the door, slamming it behind her again.

By now, most of Laurel Dorm was wide awake; all that door slamming and shouting would have wakened heavier sleepers than a group of high-strung teenagers.

"What's going on?" demanded Mrs. Hayward, coming out of her room yawning. "What's all that racket?" She moved to the top of the stairs and looked down into the empty lobby. "What time is it?"

"It's half-past twelve, Mrs. Hayward," a helpful freshman called out.

As if on cue, Angela Torres chose that exact moment to push the front door open cautiously and tiptoe in, an hour and a half past curfew. Right in front of a shocked and whispering audience of Holly Hills girls and an angry dorm mistress.

"Angela Torres! Go to your room this instant! Miss Appleyard and I will see you first thing in the morning in her office. Meanwhile, consider yourself grounded for the rest of the year!"

Under her white linen sheets, dressed in pure silk jammies, Tucker Tuckerman heard Mrs. Hayward's furious words and smiled to herself. But this was only the beginning. What was to come next would be far, far worse, worse than anything Angela Torres could imagine.

"I'm disappointed in you, Angela, very disappointed. When you came to us, you were filled with promise. I had only the highest hopes for you. But your grades are only fair, your classroom work is slipping, and now this! Breaking curfew is a serious infraction of Holly Hills rules. What are you doing to your future?"

Tears of humiliation stung Angela's eyelids. If only Miss Appleyard sounded angry instead of so sad and disappointed. That would have been much easier for Angela to bear. But the gentle reproach in those eyes made her want to throw herself into the Apple's arms and sob out her story.

But how could she tell the truth? The truth was that she had been as guilty as Pepper, had been as willing as he to dawdle, letting the golden moments trickle by like sand in an hourglass. It was only at the eleventh hour that she'd come to her senses, and by that time it was just too late. No matter what excuses she could give Miss Appleyard, Angela had nobody to blame but herself.

And not only this one guilty episode, it was an entire pattern that she was forced to look at now, a pattern of misbehavior and neglect that was suddenly clear. She'd been so proud of herself and her new popularity; now she was ashamed. Girls like Anthea Tuckerman were taken care of from the cradle, but nobody would take care of Angela Torres except Angela Torres. It wasn't Tucker's ass that was in trouble; it was Angela's. It wasn't Tucker's future that was in doubt; it was Angela's. No matter what might happen at Holly Hills, Tucker Tuckerman was safely enrolled in her great-great-grandmother's college. Nothing could touch her. Angela Torres was out there on a rope, twisting slowly in the breeze. She'd been given her chance, she'd blown it. No more scholarships for Angela Torres.

"I'm going to give you another chance, Angela, but it

must be the last one. When you return from the Thanksgiving holiday, I want to see a big change in you. Much less
frivolity and a lot more serious purpose. I want to see you
making good use of that intelligence nature has given you.
If you want to hold on to your scholarship, your grades
will have to improve dramatically. I expect to see that
happen. I'm going to make it easier for you by keeping you
grounded until the end of the trimester. That way you'll
have plenty of time to study.''

Another chance! The Apple was giving her a second
chance! Angela could hardly contain herself for joy.

"I will, Miss Appleyard, that's a promise! I'll be so
good and so smart you won't recognize me. My roommate,
Sara Grundfest has promised to help coach me in the
subjects I'm not so good at.''

"I'm glad to hear that, Angela, and happy also that
you've made friends with Sara. She's a remarkable
scholar, but a very lonely child, I'm afraid. I think you'll
be good for each other. Now run along, and think about
what I've said and what you promised. We'll wipe the slate
clean after Thanksgiving, and let us hope we can write an
entirely different story on it.''

"Listen to me, Jennifer Ripley, and listen hard. Your
future in this relationship depends on it.''

"Anything you say, Tucker.''

"I want you to go out there, as inconspicuously as you
can, and start spreading the news that Ms. Angela Torres
spent six months in jail for a real live grown-up crime. For
heaven's sake, don't tell more than three or four students,
and not all at the same time. The story will spread, but I
don't want it traced back to you, therefore to me. Have
you got that straight?''

"Yes, Tucker.''

"Good. If you don't screw this up, maybe I'll take you
home with me for Christmas. We have lots of parties and
you'll meet a great many eligible men, some of them even
at college.''

"Wow!" breathed Jennifer, awed. "I won't screw it up, Tucker."

"See that you don't. By dinnertime I want every Holly Hills girl to know that Angela Torres is a jailbird. It's got to be the topic of the week. I want them talking about it and about nothing else. But do it carefully, or you won't see a hayride or a sleigh ride or a blue blazer with a decent school crest on it until you're forty-five years old. Got that?"

"Yes, Tucker."

"Good. Now get out of here. I have an appointment with the Apple in less than thirty minutes, and I want to shower and change my clothes."

"So you see, Miss Appleyard, I wouldn't even be here telling you this, except that those earrings were my late grandmother's and of great sentimental value. The fact that they were emeralds set in platinum is of little consequence . . . except, of course, to the thief."

Miss Appleyard looked long and hard at the pale blond girl dressed so modestly in an old tweed skirt and a sweater with a rip in it. She felt wretched; she always felt wretched when something like this happened, when one of her girls betrayed her trust and the fine Holly Hills tradition.

"First, I must tell you that I am indeed sorry for your loss," said the Apple slowly. "We will do everything that we can to recover your earrings. But I must say to you, Anthea, that I have never encouraged wealthy girls to keep prized possessions with them. It's a mistake. Emerald and platinum earrings are what the law calls 'an attractive nuisance,' too much of a temptation to a weak girl who might never own anything so valuable. It's a sad truth, but so it is. I'm seriously considering banning precious jewelry from the campus entirely. Our insurance premiums are staggering enough as it is."

Tucker, with ferocious concentration, managed to produce a single tear, and allowed it to roll unchecked down her cheek.

"Don't cry, child," said the Apple sympathetically, putting one soft hand on the shabby sweater. "We'll make every effort to get your earrings back. Meanwhile, while you are still in this office, you had better telephone your parents and we'll break the news to them together without delay."

Tucker kept her face long until she was safely back in her room and out of that grungy sweater she'd been forced to borrow. Then, with nobody to see her, she broke into a broad grin. The ball had begun to roll. Angela Torres' ass was grass and Anthea Tuckerman intended to be the lawn-mower.

CHAPTER TWELVE

Mickey

When the elation of being given a second chance had worn off, depression came in to take its place. Returning to her room, Angela spent the entire afternoon there alone, trying to make some sense of what her life had become in the last few months, and how it happened to get out of her control.

Angela Torres had never been introspective, preferring to take action rather than stop and take thought, but now she searched hard into her private self, trying to come up with some answers. It wasn't easy.

She had always been inner-directed, marching to her own music, doing what she considered right and best. What strangers thought of her had mattered little. But since she'd come to Holly Hills she had changed; now she was anxious for approval from people she didn't even care much about. Somewhere along the way, she'd lost her center. Entering Holly Hills, Angela had found a new world, one filled with temptations and delights she'd never before experienced, one that exposed her to life-styles that she envied, and made her want things that she couldn't afford, not financially, not emotionally.

All her life, Angela Torres had known where she was going and what she wanted to do when she got there. Even when the trouble happened and she'd been sent away for the six months she'd served in a girls' correctional facility, it hadn't stopped her progress, only slowed it down a little. Suddenly now, at sixteen, nothing seemed certain anymore.

Sure, she'd had some good times here, some wonderful times. Life had opened up to her, introduced her to new pleasures. But did she have to surrender her own integrity to enjoy them? It was one question that was weighing heavily on Angela, and she had nobody to talk to, nobody who could help her find the answer. Even Sara, who was so intellligent and in many ways so mature, wouldn't understand what it was like to be suddenly let loose in a candy store. And if Sara didn't have the answer, who could Angela ask?

Certainly not Tucker or Pepper Tuckerman. Angela knew what their answer would be. Everything had come easy to them, had been handed to them wrapped in ribbons on a silver plate. Their expectations had always been met; it was the secret of their confidence. They were the Golden Ones, and they had precious little time for anybody who wasn't as golden as they.

Maybe it was a part of growing up, this sudden insecurity. She saw it all around her, in boys as well as girls. Sara suffered from it, and so did the Three Stooges, whether they knew it or not. It showed in their hysterical anxiety to please Tucker Tuckerman.

Even privileged boys like Lindsay Hagen and Michael Harrison were filled with self-doubt and self-consciousness. Only Tucker and Pepper seemed to be free of it. But the Tuckerman twins were both experts at hiding their feelings, presenting to the world a cool and unruffled facade, so maybe there was something underneath that gave them nightmares too.

Because Angela was having her nightmares again. She'd had bad dreams while she was "inside," which had continued for months after she got out, but gradually, they'd diminished in intensity and then, finally, stopped. Now they were back; there was no surer indication that she was deeply troubled.

The nightmare was very vivid, and it was the same one, played over and over like a tape. She was sitting in the courtroom, waiting for the judge to pass his sentence on her. As a juvenile, she'd had what amounted to a hearing, rather than a jury trial. She could see her mother weeping silently and her father fighting back his own tears. Her brothers and sisters, with their husbands and wives, sat looking grim, the girls with their arms wrapped tightly around their crying mother. Only the baby of the family, little Rosita, was absent, but even in her dream Angela knew why.

With the clarity that a nightmare gives, Angela could hear the judge's words, every syllable echoing with a hollow booming in her restless brain.

"Although I have carefully taken into consideration the circumstances involved, and although I agree that they are certainly mitigating, I find with regret that I must sentence you to one year in a minimum-security facility, with the possibility of parole after six months. We all understand that you thought you had to do what you did, but your way is not the way justice is best served. *Lex talonis*—an eye for an eye—is a dangerous path to follow, not only for the individual but for democracy and for all humankind."

And her lawyer, a young Hispanic woman from Legal Aid, standing to move that the sentence be suspended or set aside in view of the defendant's age and previous spotless record, in view of the mitigating circumstances.

The sound of the judge's gavel as he denied the attorney's motion was like the dreadful tolling of an iron bell.

In her dream Angela next saw herself in that hellhole slum of a prison they called a "correctional facility." She was wearing the regulation prison uniform, an ugly green nylon dress with no collar or belt, her hair skinned back tightly and bound by an uncomfortable heavy rubber band. All around her, angry faces, angry voices, and a loss of hope. It was there she'd taken her first smoke, unfiltered cigarettes, harsh and stinking. At least it passed the time.

Now the dream changed subtly, becoming even darker. She began to feel the same anger, the same hopelessness as those around her. What was the use? How would she ever amount to anything now or achieve any of her goals? Once a delinquent, always a delinquent. That's what they all said, not only the female guards but also the girls. You'll be back, they told her mockingly. You'll be back. You won't be able to stay out of trouble. And we'll be here, waiting.

No! Angela woke up, her heart hammering in her rib cage, her mouth dry, and her fists clenched. No! I'll never go back! But the anger and the fear stayed with her, coloring her days as well as her nights. It was this anger and fear that Sam had once helped her overcome. If only he was here to help her now! Sam was the only person who really understood her.

She had thought she was in love with Sam, still thought so, some of the time. But what did she mean by the word *love*? After all, hadn't she held him at arm's length for more than a year, only to surrender to Mickey Harrison almost at once?

For the first time in her life, Angela was feeling guilty. Inside the deepest part of her, she felt that she had betrayed her Sam, and she had to walk around with that knowledge inside. She didn't like the feeling. Guilt was another of the burdens she was carrying.

She told herself that she was free; nobody owned Angela Torres. Yet that wasn't entirely true, and she knew it. Ismail Figueroa had a rightful claim to a big piece of her heart. And now Mickey Harrison did too. Which was totally confusing. How could she love two boys at the same time? Three, if she was falling for Pepper Tuckerman, which she suspected was a distinct possibility. He was the most attractive boy she'd ever been out with. What kind of girl was she turning out to be? There were Spanish words to describe girls who were easy with their affections, and they were harsh and ugly words.

Why did life have to be so damn complicated? Everything had seemed clear before, cut and dried. Stay away from involvement here, just get your education, and keep out of everybody's face. It should have worked, but it didn't. First, she found herself involved with Tucker, then with the privileged, sophisticated life of Tucker's rich-bitch crowd. Then came the boys. Next, Angela had lost sight of what had brought her to the school in the first place—an education and a ticket out of grinding poverty and grueling monotony, a ticket to the stars.

She had dreamed of engineering school, maybe even MIT, of studying astrophysics, working with sophisticated computers and a magnificent telescope. Perhaps even an internship with one of the big boys of the aerospace industry, then—an application to NASA. More than anything, Angela wanted to be the first Puerto Rican woman to travel into space. Now, with her grades slipping as her social life blossomed, that dream seemed as remote and unattainable as it would have been when she was "inside." It was a joke, that dream, a sacrifice on the altar of cheap popularity.

Her thoughts were so heavy they weighed her down. All around her, she saw happy, laughing girls, girls relieved to have midterms over, joyful about going home for the Thanksgiving holiday. And Angela had no idea what she was going to say to her parents when she got home. They'd seen her off so filled with hope and pride—she hated to let them down.

You should have thought of that sooner, said a voice inside.

Hey, she protested to the voice. Hey, gimme a break; I'm only sixteen.

Old enough to know better.

Yes, but young enough to learn.

It was a bitter lesson Angela Torres was learning—that pleasure somehow ran up a debt that had to be paid. The wise paid it in advance, by hard work, so that they could have their pleasure as a reward. That way they avoided the heavy interest charges and penalties that the foolish incurred, those who ate dessert first and were stuck with the rest of the meal. Angela had had a great time, but she was paying for it dearly now.

"Take the best and leave the rest," Sam had advised her more than once. She'd taken the best; had she come too far to leave the rest?

While she was still trying to sort out her emotions and her guilt feelings, the phone rang for her.

"Angela?" The voice was subdued, a little sad.

"Hello, Mickey."

"I . . . uh . . . I heard about last night . . . with Pepper. Did you get into trouble at school?"

She blushed, unable to think of anything to say. A glum "yeah" was the best she could do.

"Look, I have to see you, I must talk to you."

"I'm grounded, Mickey. Probably for the rest of my natural life. I blew it."

"What about the Goldfish Bowl?"

Angela shrugged, forgetting that Mickey couldn't see a shrug over the phone.

"Angela?"

"I really don't know. Probably not."

"Look could you find out? This is really important to me. I just have to talk to you face-to-face."

Oh, terrific. He not only wants to kiss me off, he wants to see the look on my face when he does it. Rub my nose in it a little. Well, she sighed to herself, I probably deserve it. "I'll try," she said sadly. "I'll call you back."

"Don't just try, Angela, try real hard!"

Mrs. Hayward was very reluctant to grant permission to Michael Harrison to call on Angela Torres, even though the Goldfish Bowl was, technically, not part of being grounded.

"I don't approve of any of this, Angela. You heard Miss Appleyard this morning. You've been neglecting your classroom work, you don't participate in any school activities, you're not on any of the teams, yet you ask for special favors. That's not the conduct of a Holly Hills girl."

"I know, Mrs. Hayward, I've been thinking about it a lot, and I realize I've been messing up. I really apologize. When we come back after the break, I'm going to do a whole lot better. I promised Miss Appleyard and I'm making the same promise to you."

The dorm mistress looked long and hard into the girl's face, but she saw nothing of the old sullen Angela, only a sad, subdued, even depressed girl in whom the too-bright flame was now merely an ember. Mrs. Hayward felt as sorry for her as she did for the bedraggled homeless cats she was always taking in and feeding.

"All right, he may visit," she relented. "But for no longer than one hour. Sixty minutes on the dot!"

"Great!" exulted Mickey when she told him. "An hour will be plenty."

Probably five minutes would be plenty, thought Angela gloomily. She didn't bother to dress up or even put on lip gloss, just came downstairs in her oldest jeans and the inevitable sneakers.

Mickey led the way into the furthest corner of the bowl, where they sat down rather awkwardly in two lumpy chairs facing each other.

For a minute he said nothing, but looked away, refusing to meet her eyes. Then, "Angela . . ."

Great, here it comes. The kiss-off. She felt an inexpressible sense of loss which took her by surprise. Was she really so attached to Mickey Harrison?

"Angela, I have a lot of trouble with the L-word."

"The L-word?" she asked, mystified.

"You know, that word that men can't say so easily. "Luh . . . luh . . ."

"Love?"

"That's it, that's the word. Thanks. I couldn't have done it without you. I feel the L-word about you, Angela Torres, and it's breaking my heart to see you running around with that no-good Pepper Tuckerman. He's wrong for you; he'll hurt you if he gets the chance. He's hurt a lot of girls. I don't think he's capable of really feeling anything. At least, if he is, he certainly knows how to repress it. I just don't want to see you get hurt, Angela. Even if you don't want to go out with me . . . well, I can understand that . . . I think . . . but please don't let Pepper take advantage of you." Mickey blurted out the whole thing in one long breath and then stopped.

For a moment Angela just sat there, stunned. This was so different from what she'd expected to hear! She stared at Mickey, recognizing that he was waiting for some answer.

"The L-word?" she asked slowly. "You love me? Would you mind repeating that a little louder?"

"I luh . . . luh . . . L-word you." Mickey smiled bashfully. "I have ever since that first time we . . . we . . . oh, you know what I'm talking about."

"Yes, I know." Her lids dropped, and her long lashes brushed her cheek; she felt confused, embarrassed, and suddenly shy. Shyness was a brand-new feeling to Angela Torres.

"You didn't do that with Pepper Tuckerman, did you, Angela?"

She opened her mouth, suddenly angry, to tell Michael Harrison that it was none of his business, but one look at his hopeful anxious face changed her mind. It *was* his business; her involvement with him had made it his business.

"No, Mickey, I didn't. Honest. We fooled around a little, a few kisses . . . not a lot more."

His entire body collapsed in one long sigh of relief. "Are you going to see him again?"

For a moment, Angela was tempted to tell Mickey about the way she'd shoved Pepper out of his own car, but she bit back the words. It wasn't a story she wanted making the rounds at Cumberland Prep. Instead she just shook her head and said quietly, "He's history." And she meant it. She felt a new surge of strengthened resolve.

Instinctively, Mickey reached out to her, but at the last moment, before his hand could clasp hers, he remembered where they were and what the Holly Hills rules were. No intimate touching in the Goldfish Bowl. Period.

"Angela, I've missed you so much. Can we get together again, like we were before? I know you're grounded, but maybe over the Thanksgiving weekend?"

"I don't know, Mickey, I honestly don't know. I've been doing some heavy thinking about my life in the last few hours, and I can't really say I've come up with any right answers. But there are a few things I *do* know. No more playing games for me. I'm not good at them. For me, things have gotta be on the table, out where you can see them. And that goes for relationships. No more trying to make you jealous, which is what, I'm sorry to say, I was doing with Pepper Tuckerman.

"But more than that, I've gotta make up my mind if I'm a serious person or just some dumb-ass goofball. I mean, what the hell am I doing in a place like Holly Hills if I'm not getting an education? Education comes first, and I've been putting it last. Shit, I wasn't registered at some snotty college on the day of my birth, like Anthea Tuckerman. Nobody's gonna pick up the tab for me if I screw around. I've got one shot and only one shot at a future—Holly Hills is *it*!

"Mickey, I've got a lot of sorting out to do in my own head, and I can't make you any promises. Except one. When I come up with a decision, it will be an honest one, not more game playing, and you'll be the first to know. Is that fair?"

Michael Harrison's face was as serious as her own as he nodded his head. "It's fair. I could hope for more, but it's fair." Then he smiled again, that familiar grin of his. "I'm glad we talked, Angela. I'm glad I said the L-word. I've been carrying it around inside me for a long time. I promise not to push you anymore. It should be enough for you to know that I'll be biting my fingernails down to the elbows until I hear from you."

But Angela didn't return his smile. She was more serious than ever when she said, "There's something else I have to tell you, Mickey. The Thanksgiving weekend is out. I have to see my family and my . . . friends." She didn't mention Sam's name. "If . . . or when . . . we get back together, it can't be like it was. Not that it wasn't sensational, but it was too heavy. Sex complicates things; I'm not ready to handle it yet. Right now, I'd just like to get to know you better. Hey, I need to know *me* better too. When I'm older . . . maybe."

Mickey's shoulders sagged. "Wow! That's a tough one to take. But, okay, Angela, you're the boss. Whatever you want is what I want, because I want you to be comfortable with me, with *us.* "

Angela stood up. "Mickey, I gotta go. I'm grounded, remember? On probation. If I'm not back in my room in five minutes, they'll kick my ass clear out of Connecticut all the way to the Bronx. Thanks, Mickey." She took his hand briefly, more of a friendly handshake than a caress. "You're okay, you know that? *Muy macho,* in the best meaning of the word. You're already my *amigo,* my friend."

When she got back to her room, little Sara was sitting on her bed, her face tense, her eyes wide and staring.

"What's the matter?" Angela asked her hastily.

"Where have you been all day?" Sara answered the question wth a question of her own.

"Right here in this room. Why?"

"Then you don't know?" Sara's voice was strangled, as if she was fighting back tears.

"Know what?" Taking a step forward, Angela shook her roommate, a little too roughly. "What is it? Spit it out!"

Sara burst into sobs, heavy sobs that shook her small body. "Everybody in the school is saying that you went to prison once, that you're some kind of criminal. And . . . and . . ." Tears overcame her, taking her breath away.

"And what?" yelled Angela, horrified.

"And that you stole Tucker Tuckerman's emerald earrings! That you're a thief!" And Sara Grundfest threw herself full length on the bed and cried as though her heart was going to break.

CHAPTER THIRTEEN

Running Away

All the breath went out of Angela, and she had to sit down suddenly. Her thoughts went racing frantically through her head. Somehow, she didn't know how, her secret had been discovered and the whole school knew that she had served time. But a thief? *Un ladrón?* Who could say a thing like that about her?

Then her heart sank as she realized the answer to her question. Everybody. The very fact of her prison record already spoke out against her, evidence for the prosecution. Angela Torres was already in trouble, so who would take her word for it when she denied ever touching those goddamn earrings? Nobody.

What they would say was that Angela Torres had every opportunity, that she had access to Tucker's room, that she'd borrowed Tucker's clothes and therefore presumably knew where everything Tucker owned was kept.

And they'd probably say, what else do you expect from a P.R. from the South Bronx? She obviously wasn't one of *us*. Send her back where she came from.

Angela's fists clenched and her head began to throb painfully. Nausea gripped her and shook her. The humiliation was more than she could stomach. She had to do something, right away, but what? Should she run all over school, buttonholing classmates to deny the charges? How could she, when the charges were still only rumor? Or should she go to Miss Appleyard and demand to know how the rumor got started in the first place? Remind the Apple that Angela Torres' prison record had been guaranteed completely confidential?

No, she was on probation, and in no position to demand anything. She felt so helpless, she wanted to scream.

For the first time, she realized that Sara was still weeping. Sitting down on the bed beside her, Angela put her arms around the smaller girl, as she'd always done with her *pequeños* when they came to her in tears.

"Hey, hey, it's all right. Stop crying, Sara, please stop," she said rather gruffly, touched by her roomie's misery.

"No, it's not all right," wailed Sara. "How can they say those awful, horrible things about you? They're not true!" And the tears broke out again, harder than before.

"Listen, Sara. Come on now, sit up and stop crying and listen to me. Some of it *is* true."

The sobs stopped, only to be replaced by sniffles and hiccups. "It's true?"

"Yeah, some of it. Get hold of yourself, cause we've got to talk. Here, take these tissues and blow."

Wondering, Sara sat up and obeyed Angela's instructions, but her eyes never left Angela's face. "You stole Anthea Tuckerman's emerald earrings?" she asked incredulously.

"Of course I didn't!" replied Angela hotly. "I never even saw the shitty things. For all I know, they don't even exist. No, Sara, the part that's true is that I did do time inside. Six months, what they call 'easy time,' in a correctional facility for girls. They wouldn't call it so 'easy' if *they* had to do it."

"Angela, can I ask you why? I mean . . . what did you do to get sent away?"

"You mean you don't know? The whole damn school isn't buzzing with it?"

The smaller girl shook her head. "No, all they're saying is that you went to jail. Nobody knows why. But—" she broke off, unwilling to continue, unwilling to wound Angela.

"But what? Come on, Sara, out with it! How can I

stand up for myself if you don't tell me what it is they're accusing me of?''

"Well, they're saying that you probably went to jail for . . . theft." On that last word, Sara lowered her voice to a sad whisper.

Angela bit her lip angrily. "I guess that this piece of news is by now the only topic of conversation over at Cumberland. The girls probably had to take numbers lining up for the phones, right? Mickey Harrison has already heard it from six different sources by now. And Lindsay Hagen. Not to mention Pepper Tuckerman. After all, they are his sister's earrings. So if Holly Hills knows and Cumberland Prep knows, that means every damn preppie in every private school in Connecticut knows. And they believe it, right? *Right?*"

"Right," whispered Sara unhappily.

"Is that what *you* believe?"

Sara Grundfest raised her eyes to meet Angela's and shook her head vehemently. "No, it's not. I don't believe you could ever steal anything."

"Okay. Then we're all right, you and me, no matter what happens. Do you want to know why I went to jail?"

Hesitating for a moment, Sara finally nodded yes.

So Angela took a deep breath and began to tell Sara the whole sordid story. Sara started sobbing less than halfway through it and cried all the way through the box of Scotties by the time Angela's last sentence died away.

"Oh, Angela," she gasped. "What a terrible thing; I can hardly imagine it."

"No, *chica,* where you come from things like that don't happen very often. But in my world it's only too common."

"Angela, if you told that story to everybody, they'd *know* you could never be a common thief, just as I do."

"Hold it! Back off! Nobody else is going to find that out, get it? It's our secret, yours and mine and the Apple's. Now keep it that way, promise? Not even Lin?"

"Not even Lin," vowed Sara in a trembling voice. "But that's so unfair to you, Angela."

"That's bullshit; it doesn't matter about me. It's private business, family business. Not for strangers."

At that moment, a sharp rap on the door. The two roommates looked at each other, then Angela called out, "Come in."

The door opened, and Mrs. Hayward, followed by Anthea Tuckerman, came into the room. The dorm mistress's face was the picture of distress, but Tucker was as cool as a skating pond on a winter's day.

Angela Torres got to her feet and squared her shoulders. Looking Mrs. Hayward straight in the eye, she asked, "What's happening?"

"As you may have heard, there's been a rather dismaying occurrence. Anthea Tuckerman has lost quite a valuable pair of earrings, and we're . . . we're—"

"We're searching all the rooms." Tucker finished the sentence calmly.

"Beginning with ours?" demanded Angela through clenched teeth.

"Actually, no. We've searched mine already, and Stacey Underhill's, Missy Farina's, and Jennifer Ripley's."

"Coming up empty, of course."

"Of course." Tucker's cold green eyes met Angela's angry brown ones and didn't flinch.

Angela turned to Mrs. Hayward. "What if I say no?"

The dorm mistress looked startled. "Well . . . you have that right, I suppose. But . . ."

"Never mind." Angela shrugged. "Of course you can search. Take your time and get yourself a good look. We've got nothing to hide. Right, Sara?"

"Right." The smaller girl moved closer to Angela, as if to lend her support.

Instantly, Tucker Tuckerman began to paw through Angela's bureau, while Mrs. Hayward looked on nervously, Angela defiantly, and Sara went over in her head the constitutional validity of a search without a warrant, trying to pinpoint in her memory the exact language of the Founding Fathers.

Tucker closed the last drawer in Angela's dresser. There

were pathetically few possessions to go through. Then, almost casually, she turned over a pile of textbooks that sat on top of the bureau, and gasped.

"Oh, my God!"

"What is it, Anthea?" called Mrs. Hayward. "What have you found?"

Tucker turned around slowly, and held out her hand. In her palm, lovely and gleaming in the electric light of the room, sat a pair of earrings. Emeralds, set in platinum.

"These are mine, I believe." She threw the words contemptuously in Angela's face.

Now it was Angela's turn to gasp. "I don't believe it! It's not true! I never took those damn earrings, and what's more, Tuckerman here knows it!"

"Oh, Angela," mourned Sara, crushed.

"Angela, I'm afraid we're going to have to see Miss Appleyard at once. This is most distressing, most. Please take an outer garment, as the evening is quite cold."

But her last admonishment was spoken to empty air. Grabbing her denim jacket off the hook on the back of the door, Angela Torres had taken off like a greyhound, and was running down the stairs, out the front door and into the icy night.

Away. She had to get away. Nobody would ever believe her now. The hideous nightmare was coming true. They'd put her on trial and find her guilty, this time with no mitigating circumstances. They'd send her back there, back where the guards and the girls were waiting, grinning. *We knew you'd be back. We knew you couldn't stay away. This is your home; here is where you belong.*

No! she couldn't stand being locked up, never again! She needed to be free. Blindly, Angela Torres ran through the night, across the campus with its neat lawns and its evergreen holly bushes, toward the front gate.

Then where? She was 124 miles from home, with no way to get there. No, wait! In her pocket, a duplicate set of keys for her little Honda scooter. She'd turned in one set of keys to the school at Miss Appleyard's command, but to turn in both would have been stone stupid.

The bike was in the school shed, and the shed was locked, but the lock was just a flimsy padlock and the wood around it was old, weathered, rotting. It wouldn't take the Incredible Hulk to pull the disintegrating wood away and get the door open.

Her fingers were filled with splinters, but Angela Torres couldn't worry about that now. The door sagged off its hinges, and she peered inside the dark shed. There it was. Even in the dim rays of the moon, she could see the blessed little Aero shining. Lovingly, Angela wheeled it out of the shed. Did it have gas? Would it start up in cold weather? Was she stealing it? Hell, how can you steal something that's already yours? She was just going home for the holidays a day or two early, that's all. Going home and never coming back.

The bike started up at once. With a roar of the engine, she was out the gate and on the road, heading south. Free. Free at last. It didn't matter that her denim jacket was no protection against the cruel biting winds of late November. It didn't matter that her future, her career, her ambitions, everything she'd ever wanted for herself lay behind her in ruins.

Angela Torres was running away. And there was no going back.

She had gone thirty miles by the time she allowed herself a deep breath and the chance to think. There was probably no way she could make it home by the time the head mistress found the Honda Aero missing. Probably even now her parents knew what had happened, thanks to the telephone. What must they be thinking? This could destroy them. How could she convince them, or anyone, of her innocence, when the very act of taking her scooter and running away was almost a confession of guilt?

Angela was so lost in her misery that the miles melted away beneath her wheels. Almost before she'd realized how long she'd been traveling, she was crossing one of the bridges over the Harlem River into the Bronx. Anderson Avenue was only a few streets away from the river; she could be in her apartment in only a few minutes, talking to her mother and father.

But she couldn't deal with her parents now. She wasn't yet ready to face them. All Angela could think of was Sam, as though Sam were a safe harbor. If she could only find him, talk to him, then she could phone her mother and father and tell them she was all right and would be home soon. But first, she needed Sam. She needed somebody who spoke her own language, who understood her, who cared about her.

If he *did* still care for her. Holly Hills had created a gulf between them, just as he'd predicted. She'd entered an alien world and tried to pass as an alien. She'd tried to be like girls who were all face, all surface. She'd turned herself inside out to conform, and look how conforming had repaid her. By treachery. But there had been treachery on *her* part too. She had betrayed her inner self, her own integrity.

It was very late. It wasn't safe just to ride around in the near-deserted streets looking for Sam. But with any luck, she'd find him at the Hidalgos clubhouse. She turned the little Aero around and headed north a few blocks, hoping against hope.

Yes, there was the Kawasaki, parked outside, heavy chains and bike locks keeping it secure against theft. Sam was in the club.

The clubhouse was very quiet and dark, and the front door was locked. Angela hammered on it, but there was no answer. Yet Sam would never go off and leave his bike. He absolutely must be somewhere inside.

"Sam!" she hollered. "Sam Figueroa! *Dónde estás?* Sam, it's me, Angela. Open up!" If that didn't wake him up, nothing would.

In a few moments, she heard the door locks being drawn back. Then Sam's voice, very cautious. *"Angela? Eres tu de verdad?"*

"Yeah, it's really me. Let me in, Sam, I'm freezing!"

The door opened. Angela was so happy to see him that she flung her arms around him, hugging him tightly. Then, remembering her precious scooter, she turned away to bring the Honda up onto the sidewalk and into the safety of the club. As she wheeled it past him she saw for the first time that Ismail Figueroa wasn't alone in the clubhouse. Redheaded Elena Santiago was with him, and from the guilty expression on Sam's embarrassed face, Angela realized that they had been making out.

Horror and anger washed over her instantly, followed by the realization that she had no right to be jealous or possessive. Sam was only doing what Angela herself had done. There was nothing she could blame him for; they were in the same boat. How could she expect a handsome, desirable, healthy young male to remain faithful to a girl who was more than a hundred miles away and who had never shared sex with him?

But was this only a physical affair, or was Elena now Sam's girl? Angela had to know.

"Do you want me to go away, Sam?" she asked him in a quiet voice.

Shaking his head, he turned to Elena and whispered a few words to her. The redhead's eyes flashed in fury, and she whirled around, picking up her boots and her purse and a fluffy coat of possum fur, flouncing to the door, slamming it behind her, leaving Sam and Angela alone.

For a long moment, neither of them spoke. Then Sam reached out and took Angela into his arms and she dissolved in tears, sobbing against his chest and shoulder as though she'd waited too long to cry. Which she had.

"Angela! *Angelita! Qué pasa?* What's the matter?"

It took her a few minutes to recover enough to talk, minutes in which Sam just held her close, letting her cry, rubbing her back, neck, and shoulders with his strong hands, comforting her, telling Angela she was beautiful, and dear, and beloved. Finally, she managed to get hold of herself, stopped crying, blew her nose, and dried her eyes.

"Okay baby," soothed Sam, "now tell me what's been happening to my girl, and how come you turn up here at eleven o'clock at night two days early. Come sit down here and tell me everything."

He took her by the hand and led her to one of the battered clubhouse sofas. They sat down side by side, and Angela had a flash of recollection. How many evenings had they made out on this very sofa, hugging, kissing, touching? The memory of it burned, and Angela found herself very close to tears again.

Sam slipped one arm around her. "Angela, tell me everything," he said seriously.

"Oh, Sam, *me da tan verguenza.*"

I'm so ashamed. And, once more, Angela Torres burst into tears.

CHAPTER FOURTEEN

Sara Dives In

The furor over the discovery of Tucker Tuckerman's earrings on the top of Angela Torres' bureau raged for several hours, even though Mrs. Hayward summoned the Apple herself to Laurel Dorm to help restore order. Feelings ran high, and feelings were, Tucker found to her surprise, quite mixed.

As she had expected, there was an outcry against Angela, and a demand by students that she be instantly expelled. But the demand was by no means unanimous. Anthea Tuckerman was astonished to discover just how many girls at Holly Hills genuinely liked and admired Angela Torres and could not or would not easily accept the cut-and-dried evidence of the earrings. It seemed just too pat, too perfect, especially convenient coming right on the heels of the Angela-is-a-prison-rat revelation. It suddenly occurred to Tucker that she just might have overplayed her hand a tad.

But when word leaked out that Angela had not only fled the dorm but the campus, after breaking open the shed and stealing—or reclaiming, depending on who was spreading the tale—her motor scooter, the balance of opinion shifted in Tucker's favor.

Running away really did look like an admission of guilt. Many girls who didn't want to think of Angela Torres as a thief were finally forced to. You couldn't deny that Angela was gone, and the Honda Aero with her.

In the end, only Sara Grundfest stood firm on Angela's side.

And maybe Mickey Harrison, who phoned no fewer than seven times, even after Sara had spoken to him twice, telling him firmly that nobody had any idea where Angela was, even after the hall monitor had forbidden him to call after hours again. Finally the phone was allowed to ring unanswered, and eventually it stopped.

Sara lay awake all the rest of the night, torn between misery and anxiety, convinced of Angela's innocence but feeling helpless against the forces mounted against that innocence. It wasn't until four in the morning that it occurred to Sara that she wasn't as helpless as she thought. She held one card that Tucker didn't even know was in the pack. But did she have the courage to play it?

Sara Grundfest had always moused through life as inconspicuously as possible. It was easy for her to remain uninvolved and uncommitted as long as her closest and dearest companions were books. She was never in trouble, she never made waves, she was hardly even noticed, except by that handful of fine teachers who take delight in a pupil's brilliance and receptiveness to learning.

Then came Angela, bringing the fresh cold air of the world outside into Sara Grundfest's life. Angela walked tall, Angela took no shit, Angela possessed strength of purpose and strength of character. Angela Torres wasn't one of those who read about life; she lived it. For the first time, Sara began to feel that there was something out there that was attractive, a rushing stream of life that tumbled over rocks and made roaring noises, but was nonetheless exciting and refreshing. In this stream, Angela Torres was a strong swimmer, and she seemed determined to coax or drag Sara off the bank and into the water where she too could learn how to swim.

At four in the morning, Sara Grundfest realized that if she didn't act she was letting Angela down, and if she did that, she'd stand on the bank of the stream for the rest of her life, afraid to put her foot into the water.

"I'll do it," she said out loud into the darkness. "I don't know if it will do any good at all, but I'll do it." Then, as

she relaxed into sleep, a sudden thought struck her. I hope
I don't feel different about this in the morning.

"So you see, Sam, you were right about me and Holly
Hills. I never should have gone there. I should have stayed
here in the Bronx where I belong." Angela's face was more
peaceful now that she'd told him the whole story; she felt
lighter for sharing her burden.

For a moment Sam didn't say a word. Parts of Angela's
story had wounded him deeply, but he was starting to get
over that now. There were things about Angela he didn't
recognize, and it would take him a minute to sort out his
feelings and another minute to put them into words.
Reaching into his shirt pocket, he pulled out a pack of
Luckies, took one, lit it, and offered it to Angela.

She shook her head. "I'm not smoking anymore. Gave
'em up. You shouldn't smoke them, either. They'll kill you
for sure, Sam."

Sam shook his head. "You've gone through some heavy
changes, *niña*. This is a very different Angela from the
little girl I kissed good-bye. A little girl went away to
school, and a grown-up lady came back. I feel like I got to
get to know you all over again. You tell me all the bad
things that happened to you, and I say, look at the good
things. You ain't so tough anymore, you know that? You
lookin' good, and you thinkin' straight. The only thing I
don't like to think about . . . besides this Mickey dude I
wanna take apart . . . is that my Angela *es una cobarde*."

"A coward!" Stung, Angela attempted to stand up from
the couch, but Sam was stronger than she and pulled her
back down again. "Don't you dare call me a coward!"

"Why the hell not? You ran away, didn't you? You let
this Tuckerman chickie walk all over you and you never
lifted a finger to do anything about it. You picked up your
ass, threw it on the Honda, and made wheelies all the way
in from Connecticut. If that's not yellow, then suppose
you tell me what color it *is*."

The corners of Angela's lips began to tremble.

"Don't cry," ordered Sam. "You cried enough. *Valor,*

Angelita, my girl always had *valor*. Now you're smoother, you're smarter, you got better manners, but what you ain't got is the old *valor.*"

"But what can I do?" asked Angela in a near-whisper. "Anthea Tuckerman framed me, no two ways about it. But now the whole damn school knows I did time, and all of them think I took those earrings."

"Maybe if you go back, they'll think otherwise," suggested Sam softly.

"Go back!" gasped Angela.

"If you don't stand up for yourself, who's gonna stand up for you? Nobody, baby, and you shouldn't expect anybody to. You let that warped Tucker mop up the floor with you, and you quit cold. You let her get away with that shit. That's just stupid. Instead of thinking about it as round one, you threw in the towel and ended the fight. If you didn't steal those earrings, go back and prove it."

"I . . . can't . . . there's no proof." And Angela began to cry again.

Standing up, Sam pulled Angela gently to her feet. "You look beat, *querida,*" he said. "C'mon, I'll take you home. We can ride side by side on our bikes; we never did that before. C'mon, Angelita, your parents must be worried sick. What you need is a good night's sleep. Things will look different in the morning, you'll see. I'll call you first thing tomorrow."

Even in her own bed, in her own little room with the crucifix on the wall and her outgrown clothes still hanging in the closet, Angela couldn't fall asleep. She was more than just beat, she was tired to the bone, but sleep eluded her. She kept hearing Sam's taunts, *cobarde,* coward. He was right.

But go back to Holly Hills? How could she? Everybody had already decided against her, right? Judge and jury and we find the defendant guilty as charged, next case, please.

She couldn't stay here, either. Just one look at her mother's face had broken Angela's heart. They'd had such pride in her, such hopes for her, and she'd let them down. She'd let everybody down. Mrs. Deegan, her old grade adviser, Mr. Ryan, her parole officer, her parents, little Rosita, Sam, Sara. Sara? How did she get in there? She belonged in that other world, that world of strangers, Holly Hills. She'd be safer there, even with the Tuckers of this world crowding the waters like Jaws.

But there was no getting away from it. She'd let Sara down, and the Apple, and Professor Woodstein, and Mickey Harrison, and other new people who cared about her. Would she ever see Mickey again? Not in this world, maybe in the next.

But if she couldn't go back and couldn't stay here, where the hell could she go? Just get on her bike and ride away? Suddenly, that idea was the most tempting thing she could think of. Just get on that little Honda and head south, away from winter. South, Florida . . . maybe . . . sunshine, flamingos, palm trees, "Miami Vice" . . . Angela fell asleep.

Sara *did* feel different about it the next morning, but she kept a firm resolve. Today was the last day of classes before the Thanksgiving break, and it was only a half day. As soon as their last class let out, Sara, her heart pounding so loud she could hardly think, made her way to the beautiful ivy-covered main building where Miss Appleyard had her office.

"I have to see the Apple," she told Miss Appleyard's secretary, so nervous that she wasn't even aware of using the student nickname. "It's vitally important."

The Apple's secretary peered over her glasses at the terrified child. "Sit down," she said curtly. "I'll ask." She picked up the intercom phone, dialed a number, asked Sara's name, and spoke it into the phone. "Okay, you can go in."

Fighting down a rising panic, Sara Grundfest stood up and prepared to make her first wave.

"And that's what I believe," she was saying to Miss Appleyard five minutes later.

"That Anthea Tuckerman herself placed those earrings on Angela's dresser."

"Yes, when she came raging into my room to wake me up that night. I think she planted them before she turned on the light. She couldn't hide them very cleverly in the dark, but I think she was counting on nobody disturbing that pile of books before she got to them again. She took a chance, and it worked. I also think that she was behind that story that ran all over campus, about Angela's having been in jail."

The Apple sat up very straight and her eyes bored into Sara's.

"What did you say?" she demanded. "My Holly Hills girls have been talking about Angela Torres' confidential business? How on earth did information like that get out?"

"If you want my opinion . . ." said Sara tentatively. "I think one of Tucker Tuckerman's clones has been snooping around in the office files."

"But that's unheard of!" gasped the head mistress. "Clones? What are clones? Never mind, that's not important now. What is important is that a confidence has been violated, and a personal promise I made to a student was broken. This makes me very angry."

"Miss Appleyard, the girls really don't know anything. I mean, they know that Angela was sent away, but they don't know why. She told me why, and she said it was our secret—hers, mine, and . . . and yours."

Now Sara Grundfest played her strongest card, the one Tucker knew nothing about. "Miss Appleyard, you know what her 'crime' was. You know what forced her to it. So do I, and that's how I'm so certain that she could never, ever, in a trillion years, swipe a dumb-ass pair of earrings!"

Sara gasped, horrified at the word she'd used in front of one of the foremost educators in girls' school history. But the Apple was gracious enough not to notice. In truth, she was not shocked, rather a little amused to hear Angela

Torres' words in Sara Grundfest's mouth. It would take a great deal more than *dumb-ass* to disturb the composure of Agatha Appleyard.

What *did* disturb her was injustice and deceit, particularly among her beloved Holly Hills girls. She was dismayed beyond measure to learn that somebody had deliberately pilfered private and potentially destructive information and spread it all over the school just to harm Angela Torres. This whole business of the earrings had seemed shabby to the Apple from the beginning. Shabby, distasteful, elitist, and unfair. But if it were false as well . . . Miss Appleyard heaved a deep sigh.

"Well, Sara, how do you think we ought to handle this sorry mess?"

Me? Sara's mouth made an *O* of astonishment, echoing the roundness of her eyes. The Apple was asking *her*! For one split second she quailed, but then she brought back to mind the fable of the lion and the mouse. The mouse did rescue the lion when the ruler of beasts was caught in a trap. This was the chance little Sara had been waiting for as long as she could remember. The chance to be heroic.

"Here's what I think might work . . ."

"Why, yes," said Miss Appleyard approvingly when she'd heard Sara's plans. "It might indeed work. If you think that Angela would go along with it. At least it's worth a try."

She relaxed back into her leather wing chair a little and looked at Sara with some surprise. "You're a very good friend to Angela Torres," she observed.

Sara blushed under the Apple's approval. "She's been a very good friend to me."

"I'm glad to hear it. Well, I suppose that the first order of business is to get Angela's mother and father on the telephone and ask them to send Angela back here as quickly as possible. If your plan is to work, then she has to return to Holly Hills before the Thanksgiving break tomorrow morning."

Glancing at a scribbled phone number on her memo pad, Miss Appleyard placed the call herself. She spoke a few words into the phone, then hung up and turned to Sara, a look of distress on her usually composed face.

"She's not there," she told Sara. "She returned home last night to sleep but left early this morning without saying a word to anybody. Nobody has any idea where she is. Both she and the motor scooter of hers are gone!"

CHAPTER FIFTEEN

Patchie

Angela Torres and Sara Grundfest weren't the only two to lose sleep on the night of the emerald earrings. Tucker Tuckerman, who usually enjoyed the blissful repose of the comfortably privileged, tossed and turned until the crisp pure linen sheets were all rumpled and sweaty. At last, she threw them off and, careful not to wake her roommate Lolly, went over to the open window and stared at the moonlight. She didn't even notice how cold the room was until her teeth began chattering. Then she wrapped a warm cashmere robe around her, and curled up on the window seat to think.

Words danced in Tucker's head, ugly words she'd heard others using but which had never passed those chaste lips of hers—words like *sleaze* and *slime.* Desperately, she tried to stick those words to a mental image of Angela, but they wouldn't stick. They kept bouncing back to stick to Tucker herself. Exactly like that old "I'm rubber, you're glue" rhyme that children taunt each other with.

In all her sixteen years, Anthea Tuckerman had never once had a guilty conscience; what did she have to feel guilty about? Being rich hadn't been a matter of choice but of birth, but if she'd had the choice, Tucker would have chosen rich. If others were less fortunate than she, what fault was that of hers? Or what responsibility should she take? None. Even though Tucker must have heard the phrase *noblesse oblige* a thousand times, she had never thought it relevant to herself.

With no experience of a guilty conscience, it's small

wonder that Tucker had no idea why she couldn't sleep or why those awful ugly words went round and round in her brain. After all, she had done what any loyal sister would have done in her place—used any means, fair or foul, to remove her beloved brother from the clutches of Angela Torres. Where was the blame in that?

She'd lied. Anthea Tuckerman wasn't given to lying; you had to stoop to lie, and she preferred to stand erect. That's it. She was regretting the lie and the necessity for it, but she'd do it again in the same circumstances.

She'd gotten an innocent girl into trouble. Well, if Angela Torres was so damned innocent, then how come she'd been sent away for six months? The girl just simply wasn't Holly Hills material; the school would be better off without her, and Angela, rationalized Tucker, would be better off without the school.

So why couldn't she sleep, and why was she feeling as though she needed a long, hot bath, even though she'd bathed before going to bed?

What she couldn't shake was the awful suspicion that Angela Torres was a better person than Anthea Tuckerman. Angela Torres would always have a hard road to travel on foot, while Tucker breezed by in a Rolls. But Angela would have learned some useful lessons in life by the end of that road. Angela would have the satisfaction of knowing that what she'd achieved she'd achieved by herself, through her own hard work and intelligence. Nothing would ever be handed to Angela on a plate, but somehow Tucker knew that Angela Torres would never go hungry.

Whereas what had Tucker learned? How had she prepared herself for life? There were bound to be situations in which money and breeding didn't count for everything—maybe even anything! What would happen to Tucker when she couldn't throw her weight around? She shuddered and wrapped her robe more tightly around herself. It didn't bear thinking of.

She'd better get back to bed. She wanted to get up early in the morning to pack and leave for Thanksgiving as soon as possible. She felt a sudden urgency to put miles between herself and Holly Hills. When school resumed on Monday, things would be back to normal. The scandal would have been yesterday's news, Tucker would have her rightful place restored, and Angela Torres would be gone forever.

Yet Tucker remained wakeful until past five in the morning, when she fell into an exhausted sleep so profound that she was still sleeping when a freshman banged on her door with an urgent summons from Miss Appleyard.

"Yo, Tucker, you better move it on the double. The Apple is waiting for you in her office. She says, 'now!' "

Tucker groggily slipped out of bed and into the shower, which was, mercifully, free. Although unaccustomed to moving it on the double, she did manage to present herself at Miss Appleyard's office within thirty minutes.

Somehow, she was not surprised to see that little nerd of a roommate of Angela's with the headmistress. In the back of her mind, she had been expecting something like this all along.

"Come in, Anthea, and close the door behind you, please. Take a seat. If you don't mind, I'd like to ask you just a few more questions about those missing earrings."

Tucker's heart sank with foreboding, but she managed to keep a cool exterior, out of long practice. "I don't think I understand, Miss Appleyard. The earrings were returned to me, and my mother has no wish to prosecute. I've been told that the thief has run away, a clear admission of guilt. I presumed the matter was closed."

"Don't you presume any such thing," shouted Sara, jumping up with her tiny fists clenched. "And don't you dare call Angela Torres a thief!"

"Sara, please." The Apple put up a restraining hand. "We'll have no shouting in this office. Just resume your seat and remain silent, or I'll be compelled to send you back to Laurel Dorm."

Sara sat down obediently, but she continued to glare at Tucker.

"There are certain elements about the affair that make

me uneasy, Anthea. And one or two things have been brought to my attention that lead me to believe that the whole business was not as simple as it first appeared. I'd like to ask you a few questions, if I may.''

Wordless, Anthea Tuckerman inclined her head.

"Good. Now, Sara Grundfest tells me that—''

At that very moment, the office door burst open. Over the agonized protests of Miss Appleyard's secretary, Angela Torres strode in.

Three gasps met her. Indeed, her appearance would cause anyone to gasp. Her hair was standing up wildly in all directions, just as though she'd been riding a motorbike without a helmet and had pushed that little bike to its limit. Her clothes were dusty from the road, and so was her face and neck. Her eyes were angry, snapping sparks.

"I don't care if you throw me out on my ass, Miss Appleyard. First, I gotta say something. I came back just to stick up for myself, and what happens after, happens. I guess I can take anything you dish out. But I came back only to tell you that I never stole those earrings. I never stole anything in my whole life. What's more—''

"I believe you, child," interrupted the Apple quietly.

Angela's jaw dropped, and so did Tucker's, while Sara just looked very pleased with herself and with the Apple.

"You do?" echoed Angela.

"You do?" echoed Tucker.

"Yes.''

Except for the two glowing spots in the center of her cheeks, Tucker Tuckerman's pale face grew even paler, and she rose to leave the room. She had never been so terrified in her life, and the urge to run away was irresistible. Suddenly, she knew how Angela had felt only the day before, exactly how Angela felt.

"Sit down, Anthea, we're not finished yet," commanded Miss Appleyard crisply. "Angela, I have some words to say to you too. But first, there's something I want you to do, Angela. It's Sara's idea that you ought to tell the girls of Holly Hills why you were sent away.''

"No way!" yelled Angela, glaring at poor little Sara,

but one look from the Apple and she sat down hard.

"No, hear me out. I believe she's right. I think it would clear the air forever and make life here easier for you. That is, if you choose to stay with us."

Choose to stay? Tucker and Angela both stared speechless at the headmistress.

"Angela," Miss Appleyard went on more gently, "I know that this is a very difficult decision for you to make. I know you feel that this part of your life is private, but I'm afraid it's too late for secrecy. The damage has already been done, child. Being open about it can only make things better, not worse."

"Please, Angela," whispered Sara.

"You have a very loyal and devoted friend here, Angela," said the headmistress, and Sara Grundfest blushed with happiness and a shy pride. Tucker's perfect teeth nibbled unhappily at her perfect lip; nobody could ever possibly say that about her! She had no loyal or devoted friends, and was herself loyal and devoted to nobody except another Tuckerman.

"Yeah," muttered Angela gruffly, suppressing tears, "she's a good kid."

Miss Appleyard lifted Angela's chin and looked earnestly into her face. "Will you do this difficult thing? Didn't you come all the way back here to set the record straight?"

Angela drew in a deep breath and let it out slowly. "I guess so." She nodded. "I suppose you're right."

"Good. Then I think you ought to begin here and now with Anthea Tuckerman."

"Tell Tucker?"

Miss Appleyard nodded yes.

Tucker stood up quickly, but Angela pushed her back into her chair. "Oh, no you don't. You wanted to know about my life in prison, and now you're going to. So stay put and don't move a muscle. Or I'll forget I'm a lady." These words, coming from a dirty-faced, messy-haired apparition in denim, were so funny that Sara giggled.

"Quiet," ordered Angela. "All right, here goes.

"I had just turned fifteen, and I was so excited about it that I was all wrapped up in myself and not paying attention where I should have. So I didn't notice at first that my baby sister was behaving very strangely. Rosita is a good, happy little kid, and suddenly she's crying in the night and having bad dreams and just acting . . . wrong. Until, one day . . ."

"What is it, Rosita? Can't you tell Angela? Angela loves you, you know that. Come tell your big sister what's bothering you," she said in Spanish.

But the little girl just shook her head vehemently from side to side while her huge brown eyes brimmed over with tears.

Hunkering down near the child, Angela tried to put one loving arm around her for a hug, but Rosita gave a little cry of fear and pulled away.

What the hell was going on here? How did an outgoing four-year-old who was never afraid of anything or anybody turn into a mass of fear and flinching with no warning? When did this start? How come Angela hadn't seen the change before? She'd been so wrapped up in Sam that she'd paid much less attention to her sister, although, with both parents working, Rosita was Angela's prime responsibility. It was Angela who took Rosita to the day-care center every morning, and Angela who picked her up at the end of the day and brought her home. But Angela had been late several times lately, and Rosita had had to wait at the center after the other kids had gone home. Was it possible . . . ?

"Did anybody frighten you, baby?" she asked in a low voice.

The little girl shook her head no, then yes.

"Hurt you?"

Now Rosita started to cry loudly and tried to run away, but Angela caught her up in her arms, hugging her tightly, soothing her.

"It's all right, little Rosa Maria, Angela's here. Nobody's going to hurt you now. Shh, shh, don't cry, *hermanita,* Angela's going to take good care of you."

As she rocked her little sister in her arms Angela tried desperately to think. She *had* to find out what was making the girl so terrified that she couldn't talk. The darkest, most horrible suspicions came crowding into her mind. Oh, my God, what if it were true? That somebody . . . somebody filthy and evil and sick . . . had been messing around with a little four-year-old girl!

She remembered something she saw on a television news show, when a man at the Palace day-care center had been arrested for child abuse. The children, too frightened to talk, had shown the child psychologist what had happened to them, using a doll.

"Rosita, listen, sweetheart. Where's Patchie? Go get Patchie and bring her here, and we'll play a little game, okay?"

In a minute, Rosita had returned with her beloved Cabbage Patch doll.

Gently now, don't freak her, Angela told herself. "Rosita, this person who hurt you, did he touch you? Show me on Patchie where he touched you, darling."

Slowly, fearfully, the little girl picked up the doll's skirt and pointed to its private parts.

"Did he touch you more than once? Count on the doll, Rosita." One, two, three, four, five.

"You're a good girl, baby, a wonderful girl. There's nothing to be afraid of anymore. You're never going back to that place . . . not ever again. Nobody is going to hurt you anymore. Now come give Angela a hug, that's my wonderful baby. I'm going to take you next door now, and *Tía* Gracie will keep you until Mommy and Daddy come home. They'll be home very soon. Will you play nice next door? Good. Want to take Patchie with you?"

It seemed miraculous to Angela that she could so calmly take Rosita to the kindly next-door neighbor, calmly ask the favor of an hour's baby-sitting, and even smile her thanks, when, every minute, the rage inside her seethed and grew stronger and blacker. By the time she got out into the street, she was so murderously angry that her throat was filled with bile and her pulses were racing. The four short blocks to the day-care center seemed like four hundred, and it didn't occur to Angela that she didn't know the name of the abuser, not even whether it was a man or a woman.

All she knew was that she had to get her fists on somebody, make some weirdo bastard pay for hurting her little sister.

The door was locked when she got there, and it seemed that everybody had gone home. No, wait, a light at the back. With agility, Angela shinnied over the fence and into the side alley, then crept around to the back. There was an open door, and she went in.

The first thing she heard was the sound of a child crying.

Tremors gripped Angela so hard she had to press her body against the wall to stop them. Then she tiptoed along the corridor toward the light. Her heart was pounding so hard she couldn't breathe; all her energy was focused on taking one silent step after another . . . after another. . . .

The sudden hideous sight made her turn her face away; that gross, bloated man and his cowering, weeping, begging, five-year-old victim. Then, without thinking twice, Angela leaped forward, jumping on the sonofabitch's back and punching him as hard as she could.

"Run!" she yelled at the little boy. "Run away fast and find a policeman! Go get a cop and bring him here! Now!"

As the little boy's feet pounded down the corridor, Angela grabbed a handful of greasy hair and tugged hard.

Yelling furiously, the man fought back. They were alone now, struggling. Angela had had the element of surprise on her side, but surprise was over, and this man was stronger than she. She was maddened with rage, but he was fighting for his life. It was no contest. Slapping her hard, he flung her against a wall, dazing her temporarily.

Now he tried to run past her, heading for the door, but Angela grabbed on to his leg and held tightly. She'd pull that damn leg off if she had to, but hold on to him she would, until the police came.

Snarling, the man reached into the pocket of his jeans and pulled out a large pocketknife. He opened the blade and made a slash at Angela, but she dodged away and he missed.

She was quicker, but he was stronger and heavier. And armed. He slashed at her again, and this time the knife caught her shoulder and nicked it, the point going into the wall behind her, and the handle was jerked out of his huge hand. As quickly as a whippet, Angela grabbed the knife and pulled it out of the wall and jerked it around. She didn't mean to stab him, but as she turned, the knife point caught him in the side and penetrated, between his ribs. If it had been anything but a pocketknife, the monster would have been dead, stabbed to the heart.

The man staggered backward and fell, clutching his bleeding side, just as the little boy and two police officers rushed in through the door. In the blur of the action that followed, Angela lost track of time and place. She remembered very little until she stood in juvenile hall, facing arraignment, her anxious parents and a woman lawyer flanking her defensively.

"And that's the story," said Angela. "First-time offender, one year, parole in six months. My baby sister Rosa Marie is still in therapy, and still has nightmares. And so do I." She fell silent.

Sara was sniffling into a tissue, and even Miss Appleyard was touching her eyes with the lacy corner of a handkerchief. As for Tucker Tuckerman, she was crying loudly and sloppily, with no concern at all for the fact that she looked like ten pounds of crap in a five-pound bag. Her nose was bright red, her eyelids were swollen, and her cheeks were puffy. She wasn't merely crying, she was bawling, and furthermore, she didn't even want to stop, because it felt so good. Everything she had repressed for so long, all the emotions she never allowed herself to feel, came pouring out of her in a torrent of tears.

"Anthea, child, please control yourself," the Apple said in a worried tone, but Tucker kept on crying.

"Tucker, please don't," whispered Sara, with the same result. More tears.

"Hey, Tucker, cut that shit out, damn it!" yelled Angela, and as if by magic, Tucker stopped crying at once.

"I'm sorry, Angela, I'm really sorry. I was so hateful; I've never done anything like that in my life . . . Miss Appleyard, Angela didn't take those earrings. *I* did. I deliberately put them in her room to get her into trouble . . . I'm so sorry . . ."

"Pull yourself together, dear," said the headmistress gently yet firmly. "I think you ought to go and wash your face, perhaps you'll feel better."

While Tucker was throwing cold water on her swollen eyes in the Apple's private john, the other three had very little to say to one another. Angela reached over and gave Sara a big squeeze, but all she said was, "Thanks, roomie." Those two words and the hug made little Sara glow with happiness more than words could express, so she sat silent.

All Miss Appleyard said was, "As to the . . . removal . . . of your motor scooter . . . I believe you had some justification and that you've suffered enough. Holly Hills will take no action on that score. But remember, after Thanksgiving, we expect to see your grades dramatically improved."

It was a very different Anthea Tuckerman who emerged from the bathroom. Her face was still blotched and puffy, but her manner was calm.

"I apologize to all of you for my behavior just now; it was gross and very unlike me. Miss Appleyard, I think I'll collect my things and go home. By now, the car must be waiting for me. Oh, yes, one more thing, if I may. I shall not be returning to Holly Hills after the weekend; my mother will be in touch with you about withdrawing me formally. I'm transferring to another school."

Tucker and the Apple exchanged long silent glances. Tucker's eyes said, "Please let me do this; please don't humiliate me any further by throwing me out." Miss Appleyard's eyes answered, "If I go along with this, it's only because I think you've learned a bitter lesson, and may better profit by it somewhere else." The Apple was a great believer in a clean slate and a second chance.

Tucker turned to go. Her eyes met Angela's briefly, and the green ones turned away.

"Miss Appleyard, can I have five minutes alone with Tucker?" asked Angela unexpectedly. "I promise not to beat her up or knife her."

"Well, Anthea?"

Tucker Tuckerman hesitated, then nodded. The Apple shepherded Sara out of the office and closed the door gently behind them, leaving Anthea Tuckerman and Angela Torres alone together. For a long moment, the two girls just stood and looked at each other. Two girls, so very different in every way. At last, Angela grinned.

"Well, Tuck, you turned out to be a world-class full-on shit-head, didn't you." It wasn't a question.

"If you say so," answered Tucker quietly. "I'm sorry, Angela, and I've done the best I could to make it right. But you do understand that I couldn't possibly remain at Holly Hills."

"If you say so," answered Angela quietly. "I know it would take bigger *cojones* than you've got. But let that pass. You know what I'm sorry about? That we couldn't be friends, real friends. If you weren't so damn spoiled by that strawberries-and-cream life of yours, we might have made one dynamite team. Because you're not all bad, Tucker Tuckerman. You're smart and you're funny and you're cool. I learned a lot from you, whether you know it or not. A lot about grammar and manners and style. And something else, too. I learned to think before I open my mouth, and not to go off half-cocked. I learned that it's stupid to walk around with a chip on my shoulder, that I can have some damn good times if I just keep my eyes open so I can see it coming.

"Sam always told me to take the best and leave the rest, and he was right. I took a lot of the best of you, and I discovered something I never thought possible—I'd rather be me than you. I feel sorry for you, Tucker. You've got no backbone. Even with all the breaks you get, even with all the special privileges, and all your stooges running your errands, I'm better off than you are. I'm not afraid of getting my feet wet, and I can care about somebody for what he or she is inside, not because of looks or what his father does for a living. Maybe I won't have as many friends as you'll have, but they'll be better ones than yours."

Tucker's eyes dropped, then lifted to look Angela frankly in the face. "I think so too. I wish things had turned out different. Because I learned a lot from you, too, Angela Torres, and I'm glad that you'll carry a piece of me with you. Will you think of me sometimes?"

"Are you serious? Every time I see a three-hundred-dollar cashmere sweater, I'll remember Tucker Tuckerman. 'Course, with you gone, that won't be so often."

The two girls laughed, sharing a moment. "We had some good times," said Tucker nostalgically.

"Yeah, before I went out on a date with your brother. What did you think I was going to do to Pepper? Paint him dark brown and make him talk in Spanish? Being Puerto Rican isn't contagious. Believe me, Tucker, if any girl makes a move on your twin brother in the future, let it be. Pepper Tuckerman's some piece of work, and he can take care of himself."

"Yes, well, the car's probably outside by now."

"Right. Can't keep the limo and the chauffeur waiting."

"Angela dear, never call it a limo, it's a car. And the 'chauffeur' is always called the 'driver.' " And Anthea Tuckerman raised her aristocratic chin, just a little.

"Thanks for the tip, Tucker. It'll come in real handy in the Bronx."

"You won't always be in the Bronx, Angela, and you know that as well as I do. Send me a postcard from Saturn."

"Count on it."

" 'Bye, Angela Torres."

"*Hasta luego,* Anthea Tuckerman."

CHAPTER SIXTEEN

Dear Sam

Dear Sam,

Sorry I didn't phone you this week, but I'm cramming hard for my finals, and I've hardly stuck my nose outside a book long enough to grab a sandwich. The studying is going well though, thanks mostly to Sara. She says to tell you hi, and that she and Lin are a real hot item. (Actually, what she said was, "Tell Sam hello for me, and Lindsay sends his regards," but it amounts to the same thing.)

Christmas was just wonderful, and I'll never forget it. I wear the locket all the time, even in bed (no dirty remarks, *por favor*). But the best thing about the holiday was not all the great presents, but getting to spend so much time with you, and getting to have those heavy talks. They meant a lot to me. Still do.

I'm glad you're seeing things my way. Besides the fact that nothing makes me happier than getting my own way, I'm so thrilled that you're going back to school and I want to tell you about it every damn day. College is where you belong; college is what my heart is set on, and it's an experience I want to share with you. I don't know if we have a future together, Ismail Figueroa, but I'd like to think we do. But it wouldn't be much of a future unless we were equal. I'm going to run as hard and as fast as I can to get ahead, and I don't want to leave you behind. I want you running right up there with me. Why should you eat my dust or anybody else's? You got the brains for becoming just about anything you want to be.

Gotta close now, because Sara is making terrible faces at me, and I have to get back to Mr. Textbook or she'll deck me. She's getting pretty damn scrappy these days, ever since Lin asked her to go steady. I think I've created a Frankenstein.

Looking forward to the spring break.

Love,
Tuya Angelita.

"Torres. Angela Torres! Telephone."

Angela got up and stretched; her shoulders were aching from long hours of study. "Coming."

On her way to the phone, she ruffled little Sara's mop of hair. These days, Sara always wore it loose.

"Hello?"

"Hey, darlin', it's Mickey."

"Mickey, amigo, what's happening?"

About the Author

Leonore Fleischer is the author of AGNES OF GOD, BENJI, ICE CASTLES, ANNIE, FAME, STAYING ALIVE, HEAVEN CAN WAIT, A STAR IS BORN and THE ROSE, HEARTS & DIAMONDS, and THE FOUR JESSICAS. She lives in New York with her son and cat. The cat has four other cats.